Shadow H
Pre

The Twelve
Days of
Christmas

A Horror Anthology

A. Partridge in a Pear Tree
Mark MJ Green

December 1ˢᵗ

"Jesus Christ, I am fucking sick of this bloody movie!"

Sarah's yell of frustration rang out, her breath misting in the cold December air as she threw open the back door. It swung widely, rebounded off the brickwork and returned, hitting her on the knee. "Ow! Fucking hell!." She kicked the door angrily, dodging outside before it could swing back and hit her as she stormed into the garden. Her husband, Daryl, scampered out behind her. He was a thin man whose skinny frame made his limbs look over long, almost spidery. He made a grab for the object in her hand. "C'mon, Sarah. Babe. Give it back, yeah?"

She raised her arm, holding up a disc-shaped object, fully prepared to hurl it into the snow-covered garden. One side bore a picture of the actor Steve Coogan and the words Alan Partridge: Alpha Papa. The back of the disc was silver, but the sunlight reflecting from its surface created a myriad of rainbow colours that danced and gleamed. "No!" she shouted back at him, another plume of breath angrily huffing forth like an angry ghost. "I'm sick of it. Every bloody day, all you do from the moment you get home is put this fucking stupid movie on. I'm sick of it. We're sick of it."

"Oh, babe, don't bring your mother into this." Daryl lowered his voice as soon as he spoke, whispering the last few words as if his mother-in-law could hear them from where she lay nestled under blankets in her room that smelled of medication and rot.

"My mother is as much a part of this house as you are. More than you because she can't help being bedridden, whereas you choose to be a lazy, worthless, good for nothing! All you care about is this fucking movie!" Sarah waved the disc in the air, causing the colours to shift and scintillate, a multi-hued refraction dancing across her face. Daryl would have found her beautiful in that moment if he didn't fear and hate her in equal measure.

"It's not all I care about," Daryl whined. "I care about you . . . and your mum, but that movie cheers me up. It's the only thing that -"

Sarah's harsh voice interrupted him. "Only thing that what? Huh? The only thing you care about in your lazy, worthless existence?"

In an unexpected display of bravado, Daryl puffed out his thin pigeon chest and stood up to his wife. "Yes. It is the only thing that brings me any joy. I work all day to keep a roof over our heads. I work extra hours so we can afford to have" - his voice lowered to a hissing whisper - "your mother living with us, and what do I get? Nothing. You nag and complain and spew horrible things at me, and that, that movie, is the only pleasure, the only glimmer of happiness I can find."

Daryl's face was flushed, although, rather than an angry red, it had more of an embarrassed shade of pink. Tears had leaked from his eyes, leaving shiny roads down his bony cheeks, and a small wobbly line of snot dangled from a nostril until he sniffed loudly, and it scurried back inside its home.

Sarah, on the other hand, was livid. Anger was building inside her with so much force she trembled. Her body had become so hot from her escalating fury that she appeared to be spouting smoke from her pores as her body heat condensed in the chill air.

"Oh, you spend all day at work, sure enough, but don't you dare pretend to be so altruistic with me. You do it to keep away from your house. From your family. And when you come home, all you do is watch this stupid fucking movie!" She raised the disc again, the tip of her thumb and remaining fingers around the edge, causing Daryl to worry she might get fingerprints on it. "You don't do a damn thing around here to help out!" Sarah yelled.

"That's not true," Daryl's voice had lost its earlier bravado, rising in pitch and mingling with his tears to become a whiny sniffle. "I spent all weekend wiring in the Christmas lights like you asked me."

"Oh, bully for you. You climbed a ladder and hung some lights up. Whoop-de-fucking-doo, Daryl. How bloody helpful of you. Did you even test them to make sure they work? Did you?"

"Well. . . no, but,"

"No. Of course, you didn't. They probably won't work, or worse, they'll set the house on fire."

And with that, the minuscule glimmer of bravado that Daryl had felt earlier raised its head once more. The ember of manliness sparked and burned. It took the need to stand up to his wife, wrapped it in a mesh of anger and stupidity, and before he could stop himself, it caught, ignited, and his words were out in the open. "Maybe it should burn down," he said.

"Maybe it should burn and take you and your bitch of a mother with it."

Sarah's mouth gaped open; her breath became trapped in her throat as, for once in her life, she became lost for words. Daryl, on the other hand, had plenty to say. "You hear me, you old bag?" He tilted his head upward, shouting toward the upper window in the hope his words would carry through to the old woman who was no doubt snoring vilely in her blanketed cocoon. "You fucking hear me? I hope you burn! I hope you, the house and my evil cunt of a wife all - ."

Daryl's words ended mid-sentence. Something was caught in his throat, and he found himself unable to breathe. His jaw quivered, trying to close and then open as if it could somehow chomp at the air and pull it down his throat, but the blockage that had neatly severed his windpipe was lodged firmly in place.

Sarah stared in shock. In her rage, she had lashed out blindly, not even thinking about what she was doing or what she was holding, and now Daryl was standing there, eyes bulging, mouth gaping and a Blu-ray disc jammed into his throat. There was surprisingly little blood; the disc, having sliced into him with clean efficiency, had severed his trachea and was now blocking the flow of air. Sarah watched in horrified amusement as Daryl's face went from its usual shade to a more pleasing icy blue. His eye's which had been rotating in their sockets, suddenly focused on Sarah, and she gave him an apologetic shrug as his body toppled to the ground.

There was a muffled 'floompf' as Daryl fell lifelessly into the snow, sending a small cloud of fresh powder dancing and sparkling into the air.

Looking down at her husband's corpse, Sarah struggled to find words that truly expressed her feelings on the matter. After a moments silence, she finally settled on two that seemed apt. "Oh, fuck."

*

Leaving Daryl where he had collapsed and now lay leeching his body heat into the snow that formed his deathbed, Sarah entered the house, closed the back door, and headed upstairs to check on her mother.

Mama Agnes' room was a strange contrast of light and shadow. The curtains were open, letting in the morning sun, yet somehow, the location of her bed left her hidden in a wispy cloak of shadow. Her face, at present, was turned away from the door and toward the window leaving Sarah unable to see whether Agnes was awake or not.

"Mum?" Whispered Sarah. Unlike her weak-minded husband - make that late husband - Sarah kept her voice quiet due to not wanting to disturb or frighten her mother, not out of some bizarre and unexplainable fear.

The room held a sickly-sweet odour, a mixture of medication, cabbage farts, urine, and lemon-scented cleaner. Sarah tried not to wrinkle her nose against the smell out of respect for Agnes. Unlike that idiot Daryl who would pass the doorway and mumble, "I smell dead people." He was such a buffoon of a man. She should have listened to her mother and never gotten married.

"Mum?" she repeated.

Slowly, her mum's wrinkled visage turned to face her. Agnes' eyes had a sunken look, as if her skull was sucking them inward, but despite that, and the shadows that seemed to embrace her, there was a twinkle of alertness gleaming in them. Agnes' once thick, white curls had begun to thin, becoming wispy and translucent, leaving the emaciated flesh of her skull visible. Similarly, her face had a gaunt look about it, and yet her colouration was one of health rather than the expected greying pallor of a feeble elder on their final graveward descent.

"Hello, Sarah, dear." The voice of Agnes, while having a raspy, wheezing quality, also carried strength. Another of Daryl's so-called 'jokes' unwillingly popped into Sarah's head as she recalled him referring toher mother as resembling Emperor Palpatine from Star Wars. Ugh. Why was she even thinking of that idiot man and his childish ways?

"Hi, mum. Are you ok? Can I get you anything?"

"Oh, thank you for asking, Sarah, dear. Just a cup of tea and some biscuits will be fine."

"Ok. Would you like bourbons or custard creams?"

"Hmm?" Agnes mulled it over. "Why not a couple of each, eh? You only live once, or so they say." Agnes smiled, showing perfectly straight, white teeth that, despite expectations, were all her own rather than dentures.

"Ok, I'll be back in a bit with them." She turned to leave when Agnes' voice halted her.

"Sarah, dear?"

"Yes, mum."

"You need to bury it."

"Pardon?"

"The ground under the old pear tree isn't as frozen as the rest of the garden. Take it there and bury it. Do it quickly before the snow starts to fall."

"Mum? I don't understand. How. . .?"

Agnes smiled. "Sarah, dear. Is my cup of tea ready yet?"

"Oh. No. Not yet. Sorry mum. I'll get it done now."

"Thank you, dear."

Confused, Sarah left the room.

*

After making Mama Agnes her cup of tea of biscuits (and treating herself to a cheeky custard cream), Sarah donned her winter coat, hat, scarf and gloves and returned to the back garden. Agnes' earlier words about burying it under the pear tree were still undulating in her mind. She hadn't repeated the phrase when Sarah took her the tea; all she had said was a simple, "Thank you, Sarah, dear," followed by a cryptic sounding, "It's going to snow in a few hours."

Sarah had tried to broach the subject once more, but her mother had turned away to stare out the window whilst dunking biscuits into her tea and devouring the soggy mess.

Now that she stood outside, Sarah realised her mother's prediction about the weather may have been right on the button. The sunlight from earlier had dimmed, veiled by a thin covering of grey clouds which seemed to have replaced the more familiar blue of the sky. There was a strange hue to it as well, a dash of pink or purple that stained the heavens ominously.

Daryl, unsurprisingly, hadn't moved from his prone position. All that had changed was his flesh now closer resembled the alabaster tint of the snow it was pillowed against.

Heading to the shed, Sarah was relieved and annoyed to discover that Daryl still had not gotten around to replacing the lock. The wood the hasp was affixed to was old and rotten, and the screws had pulled free, leaving the door unsecured. Dragging it open, Sarah grabbed a shovel and trudged to the old pear tree. Her booted feet sank into the snow as she walked, and she cursed with each step, the unruffled snow crunching and squeaking as she waded through it. Strangely, there did seem to be a lot less of the stuff under the tree. What made it odd was that the pear tree was deciduous; its bony limbs were barren of leaves. There shouldn't have been anything to lessen the fall of snow, yet only the thinnest carpet of it coated the ground beneath the denuded branches. Despite the lack of powder and the enigma of Agnes' words, Sarah still expected the earth to be frozen and compacted. Experimentally, she placed the shovel's blade to the ground and pushed a booted foot against it. It sank into the soft ground, almost as if the soil was eager to swallow it.

Sarah yelped, stumbling backwards. The shovel remained upright, the blade buried in the earth, the handle jutting upward, reminding her of a grave marker.

Tentatively, she approached the handle, slowly reaching a hand toward it as if she feared it would somehow take form, the wood shifting into something serpentine that would wrap around her hand and pull her into the cold earth.

Her fingers made contact.

Nothing happened.

It was a shovel in the dirt, nothing more.

Sarah let out a nervous giggle that sounded more maniacal than mirthful. She looked around as if somehow expecting a figure to be skulking somewhere, watching her, ready to pounce and arrest her or mayhap to threaten to inform the authorities. As expected, the garden was silent and empty of all but Daryl's icy corpse and a few inquisitive sparrows that flitted to and fro. For once, she felt grateful for Daryl's idleness, the conifers surrounding their garden were tall, overgrown and unkempt and obstructed all from view.

Satisfied that she was unobserved, Sarah began to dig.

It took less time than Sarah had expected, the shovel sliding easily through the soft earth. She did not dig too deep, stopping when she got to around the four-foot mark and wondered if she should have dug deeper, but in all honesty, who would search in the garden for Daryl anyway? Whilst she had laboured, she had allowed her mind to wander and had resolved upon an idea. It was to do nothing. No need to report Daryl's disappearance when she could bag up some of his clothes and a few other items, dispose of them and change her Facebook status to display, 'It's complicated.' If anyone inquired, she kicked him out for being a deadbeat. Simple.

If he wasn't reported missing, in theory she should be fine. The police would never come knocking on her door, and even if they did, there was nothing to disprove her words.

The only difficult part of the disposal process was moving Daryl's corpse. It had sunk through the snow and became frozen to the lawn. Sarah had to lift his limbs to free them from the ground, and the ripping sound each one made as the frigid grass relinquished its grasp made her shudder. Eventually, she managed to free him enough to drag him over to the hole she had dug and drop him in.

The task of covering him up didn't take long.

She put the shovel back in the shed and was back in the house when, five minutes later, it began to snow.

*

It was only just past midnight, Santa Clause had emptied his sack, and Gerard was in the process of doing the same thing. He had Sarah bent over, face down upon her crumpled bedsheets, as he hammered into her from behind. Sarah had been trying to keep the noise down, not wanting to disturb her mother, but she was finding it difficult as her orgasm approached. She could hear Gerard grunting with each thrust, his guttural sounds rumbling in time with each slap of flesh as his groin met her buttocks. God, she should have done this ages ago. She and Gerard had been flirting for a while but had never taken things to the next level. Their relationship resigned to using only their hands or mouths on one another, but with Daryl finally gone, Sarah felt more at ease with giving in to her carnal desires. Stupid how being married to such a weak-willed creature had kept her from straying too badly. She hadn't seen what she and Gerard had been doing as cheating, not really, but now. Oh, fuck. Now, it was beyond amazing. The only time she had experienced anything close to an orgasm with Daryl was when she dealt with her own needs. His sexual prowess had been to lay back, leave Sarah to climb on top and then, after a minute, he would finish, and she would be unsatisfied. Daryl would go for a shower, and Sarah would scroll through porn sites to find something she could pleasure herself to. With Gerard, things were different. They had been in so many positions that she sometimes ached for the entire day afterwards. Not to mention how good her orgasms were. She hadn't realised how sexual release could be so much more intense with a suitable partner than anything she could produce herself. Like now. She could feel her body quaking and rippling as it drew near to climax; her vaginal wall tightened, clamping around Gerard's length as a shuddering orgasm had her crying out, and she felt Gerard doing the same, breathlessly calling her name as he released inside of her.

Outside their door, Mama Agnes' eyes glinted in the darkness. A sneer pulled at her lips as she muttered quietly. "Ready now. A new life is here, an old death is needed. Not long. Not long." She strode purposefully back to her room, entered her small en-suite and began washing her hands. Mud coated her fingers and swirled down the plughole as she applied soap to her hands, scrubbing them clean.

*

Christmas morning was a busy one. After Sarah and Gerard had washed and dressed, Gerard began helping with dinner - cleaning and cutting vegetables - whilst Sarah washed and dressed her mother. They had had a chairlift installed, although Agnes didn't use it very often, seeming to prefer the solitude of her room. Today, with Gerard's help, Sarah loaded her mother into the contraption and sent her downstairs so her mother could join them for Christmas dinner.

They seated Agnes at the head of the table whilst the two of them finished cooking dinner. Occasionally, Agnes would mumble something along the lines of, "Sarah, dear. Is my cup of tea ready yet?" before falling back into silence. It wasn't until Gerard put a placemat before the elder and lay the cutlery in position that she did something unexpected. Her hand shot out, grasping hold of Gerard's wrist with what felt like a bony claw and leaning toward his face, her breath a mixture of minty toothpaste and death. "Needs a bit more power, dear. A bit more life. Switch on the outdoor lights, would you? Give things a little jolt."

Gerard tried his best to hide the look of panicked revulsion from his face as Agnes stared deep into his eyes. Her grip on his wrist tightened and caused discomfort. It wasn't until Sarah spoke that she seemed to relax and release him from her skeletal grasp.

"Mum? Oh my God, Mum. I.. . I don't think I've heard you speak so well in ages." She turned to Gerard, who was rubbing at where Agnes had grasped his wrist. "Did she say something about turning on the Christmas lights?"

"Erm, I think so?"

Sarah pointed to a pair of wall switches by the back door. "The switch for them should be there, the one on the left." If Daryl wired the damn things correctly, she added quietly to herself.

Walking to the switches, Gerard flicked on the leftmost one.

The electricity coursed along the wire, each festive light illuminating briefly in a chain reaction toward the end, where the wire had been stripped of insulation and wrapped around a metal spike driven into the ground under the old pear tree. The glow on the lights oscillated rapidly before a discharge of electricity pulsed into the metal and cascaded into the ground. Bolts of blue/white energy crawled like hungry worms, burying into the earth and writhing over Daryl's partially rotted form. His limbs twitched and convulsed, the disc in his throat began to rotate, and he began to dig his way to the surface.

As the energy resurrected Daryl's decomposing form, the outside lights exploded in a shower of sparks and brightly coloured pieces of glass, followed by a bang from within the house as the fuses blew and the power went out.

The house wasn't in complete darkness. Enough grey light filtered through the windows to create a murky luminance. Sarah, however, couldn't stop her anger from boiling over. "Jesus Christ! I should have known that idiot didn't connect the bloody lights properly. Even from the grave, he mocks me with his bloody incompetence."

"Wait, what?" said Gerard. "Grave? I thought you said you kicked Daryl out?"

"I . . . I was speaking metaphorically. He's dead to me, is what I meant."

"Erm, I think I might like to go home now."

"What?"

"Knock, knock," said Mama Agnes.

Both Sarah and Gerard turned to look at the old woman. "Knock, knock," she said once more.

"Mum?"

"Who's there?" answered Gerard, unable to stop himself from replying as if she were telling a joke.

With a crash, the back door was flung open with such force that it tore away from the bottom hinge. In the rectangular space that led outside and swirled with cold air and sparkled with flakes of shimmering snow stood Daryl. Or rather, what remained of Daryl.

The winter temperatures had kept him reasonably well-preserved. From the front, he resembled his usual self, more or less. His complexion had a pale discolouration, and crumbs of dirt decorated his shoulders and head. Due to the freezing temperatures, most creatures that dwelled in the ground had been at rest, therefore, not many had feasted upon him. His clothes hung looser than they had in life, and his skin had a taught, leathery look that appeared to have pulled back his lips, leaving his teeth exposed in a repulsive grin. One of his eyes seemed to have vanished completely, leaving the dirt-filled hole in his skull visible. The remaining orb was withered, like a piece of dried fruit. On his right side, where he had lain, Daryl's skin was stained an unpleasant purplish-black and bore a grotesque swollen appearance. The stench that drifted in with Daryl as he stepped into the kitchen was that of fresh dirt and rotten meat.

The disc was still lodged in his throat, and when Daryl opened his mouth, causing a clatter as two of his teeth fell to the floor, it crackled with electrical energy, spinning faster and faster. From his dirt-infested and rotting mouth, a voice that sounded like that of the character of Alan Partridge emanated from Daryl. "There. He's back on his feet."

"Daryl?" uttered Sarah.

"I really should be getting home," mumbled Gerard as he began cautiously backing out of the room.

Agnes pointed a withered finger at Gerard's retreating figure. "Daryl, be a dear and kill him, would you?"

Without hesitating, Daryl lunged toward Gerard, who screamed, allowing Daryl to grab the invitingly open jaw with his rotting fingers. Four of his digits slid into Gerard's mouth, wrapping over his teeth. His thumb dug behind the mandible, pressing against the soft dimple of skin. Gerard clamped his teeth upon the undead fingers that had invaded his mouth and instantly regretted his decision as his incisors cut into the cold, dead flesh. Pieces of withered skin broke apart, falling over his tongue and coating them with a taste like rancid bin juice. Unable to stop himself, Gerard's stomach rebelled, and he vomited as the ungodly flavour assaulted his taste buds. Unfortunately, the combination of bile, stomach acid and the remains of a mince pie he had washed down earlier with a glass of brandy did nothing to improve the vile taste sensation he was currently experiencing.

Daryl shoved his thumb through the soft flesh behind Gerard's jawbone. Blood pooled outward, coating the rotten digit in crimson warmth, the coppery taste of fresh blood merged with that of Daryl's decomposing body and the mouthful of regurgitation. Gerard let out a thick, bubbly gurgle of pain and disgust as the combined effulgence filled his mouth, trickled down his throat and slopped from the corners of his lips. Phlegmy strings of clotted puke dangled from his nostrils, and he struggled to breathe as Daryl raised his other hand, grasped Gerard's shoulder to brace himself, and pulled.

Gerard's jaw dislocated with a crack, followed by a horrific tearing sound as the skin of his cheeks and jowls stretched taught before tearing apart in a spray of blood and flesh. There was a soggy spatter of fluids as the vomit that was in Gerard's mouth poured from the rent in his face and carpeted the floor. Chunks of flesh joined the mess creating scarlet streams of blood that swirled in the yellowy-green bile as it ran from Gerard's ruined kisser.

There was a thud as Daryl dropped the gore-streaked jawbone. Next, he reached up to grab his victim with both hands. From the horrific wound, Gerard's tongue flapped and writhed like an eel trapped on a fisherman's hook. There was another crackle of energy from the disc lodged in Daryl's throat. Once again, the voice of Steve Coogan's character of Alan Partridge, crackled from his mouth. "I gave her a ruddy big kiss she won't forget in a hurry." Leaning forward, Daryl bit into the twitching muscle. Black, rotten teeth buried into the tender piece of meat, and with only the slightest bit of pressure, Daryl tore it free.

Stunned by what was going on, Sarah could do nothing more than gape in horror as her lover was mutilated by the freshly risen corpse of her deceased husband, whilst Mama Agnes grinned and clapped her hands in glee.

A scarlet waterfall pumped from the severed tongue stump. Unable to devour the morsel in his mouth due to the blockage caused by the disc, Daryl let it tumble wetly to the floor. There was another blue crackle as the voice of Alan Partridge rang out. "Some people say it's more hygienic than a handshake."

Daryl jammed his fist down Gerard's throat. His windpipe bulged alarmingly as Daryl pushed his arm farther and farther inside, not stopping until his shoulder scraped against Gerard's upper teeth. Grabbing a fistful of innards, Daryl yanked his arm out as hard as he could, his cadaverous hand dragging out a steaming coil of intestines. Like a stage magician

Daryl drew them out of the cavernous hole in a wet, slippery coil, leaving them dangling from the rent in Gerard's face, giving him the impression, he had been trying to eat a huge plateful of spaghetti.

Satisfied that his wife's lover was dead, Daryl released his grip, letting the body collapse to the floor.

He looked at his gore-smeared hand. "Who's to say you can't get shit on your fist?"

Sarah remained frozen by the grisly tableau until Agnes ceased her applause and spoke to her. "Sarah? Sarah, dear?"

On a neck that felt uncomfortably stiff, Sarah turned to face her mother.

"Mum?"

"Your turn now."

"Wha-?"

In the short time Sarah had looked away, Daryl had crept up to her. He grabbed her roughly by the shoulders and slammed her back flat against the table, scattering cutlery and festive table decorations. One hand pinned her against the hard wooden surface whilst the other pried her jaws apart.

Rising stiffly from her seat, Agnes opened a drawer, retrieved a razor-sharp carving knife and stood over Sarah's struggling body.

"You've really wasted your time on this earth, Sarah, dear. Time to let someone else take the wheel."

Before Sarah could react, her mother sliced her own throat.

The blood cascaded down, pouring over Sarah's face and into her mouth as she choked and sputtered against the torrent of coppery fluid, unable to turn away due to Daryl's relentless hold.

As the last of the fluid trickled from Agnes' throat, the old woman collapsed upon herself, nothing more than a dried husk.

Sarah had ceased struggling. Her tongue slid from between her lips, licking at the fresh blood.

Daryl relinquished his grip.

"Thank you, Daryl, dear," Agnes said.

The zombified Daryl respectfully backed away a few steps.

"I always worry a little bit during a soul transference," Agnes told him, rising from where she lay on the table. "It's that moment of cutting my own throat that causes me a slight panic about what would happen if it didn't work this time."

The voice of Alan Partridge crackled from Daryl. "I've had one panic attack in a car wash,"

"Yes, enough of that nonsense I think," said Agnes, and she ripped the disc from Daryl's throat. "Be a dear and dispose of this infernal thing," she said, holding it out for him. "Then, clean up this mess you made."

Nodding sadly, Daryl wandered through the broken door and shuffled outside, back to the pear tree.

With surprising tenderness, he slid the hole in the centre of the disc over a branch of the pear tree. He may not have been capable of shedding tears, but a beetle emerged from the dirt-filled empty eye socket giving a putrid version of the same thing.

Turning away, he headed inside to tidy up, leaving the disc swaying gently in the cold air.

In the kitchen, Agnes, now possessing the body of what used to be her daughter, rubbed the area just below her stomach. She had been a mother many times before and would be one again.

TWO TURTLE DOVES

Renn White

One

I can remember the exact moment that I saw it, sitting there on the shelf of my local antique shop. I knew then that it was special. It called out to me, almost beckoning me to steal it away from prying eyes.

As I made my way slowly toward the small cherry wood box, the detailed carving caught my eye, two turtle doves sitting upon a branch, their heads turned to face one another with such love and compassion that it seemed as though they were one creature.

"Its's a lovely piece, isn't it?" the old man behind the counter smiled, revealing a mouth of rotten deep brown stained teeth one would only get from years of neglect and smoking. "A truly lovely piece."

"I'll take it," I found myself saying, without even enquiring what the price was and before I knew it, I was heading back home with the box hugged tight against my chest, little knowing that this box would make this Christmas season unforgettable.

This box was to be an anniversary gift for my wife, after all the fifth anniversary was supposed to be a gift of wood and this was perfect. I had the perfect hiding spot under the bed, and I rushed upstairs the moment that I entered the house, in fear she would catch a glimpse. I needed to keep it secret for now, hidden out of site where only I knew to look.

We went about our evening as normal; dinner, tv and then a glass or two of wine before making our way upstairs to the bedroom. As I settled down for the night, I couldn't help but think of the surprise hidden under the bed. It was as if I could feel the grain of the wood, smell the sweet cherrywood and feel each intricate stroke of the engraved turtle doves.

I must have fallen asleep shortly after climbing into bed as I awoke in pitch-black darkness to the sensation of hands caressing their way up my legs.

Kate always did love a good fumble in the dark and tonight it seems she was ready for some fun. Shifting slightly, I moaned as a jolt of arousing energy coursed through me. A high-pitched snort from beside me snapped me out of the moment and glancing to the side I saw her eyes closed in the half-light. Just my luck; she was getting frisky in her sleep.

With a frustrated sigh I rolled over and soon drifted back to sleep, but the dreams that followed were filled with lust and violence, most likely brought on by the movie we had watched earlier that night.

TWO

The following day I set myself up in the office to work from home, but all I could think about was the box still hiding under the bed upstairs.

What if Kate was to go snooping, look under the bed and find it? Was my hiding place too obvious?

Would she love it? Hate it?

Maybe she'd think it was a bit of trash I had found by the side of the road and brought home.

I needed to look at it once more just to make sure I had picked the right gift. One little peek and I would get myself started with work, that was all.

I just had to wait until Kate left for work.

Twenty minutes felt like hours and finally I heard Kate walking down the hallway toward the office.

"Do you need anything grabbing while I'm out, babe?" she asked leaning around the door and smiling at me, instantly snapping me out of my thoughts.

"The box" I found myself saying almost as if I had no control over my own vocal chords, then seeing the look of confusion upon her face, I got up from my desk and gave her a kiss on the cheek. "I meant a box of tea bags…have a great day at work and I will see you when you get home, miss you already."

I watched as she walked out of the house and down the garden path before I rushed up the stairs, almost sprinting across the landing to the bedroom, scrambling across the floor to grab the box out from its hiding place. I promised myself I would only look at it for a few moments and then find a better place to hide it before Kate came home and caught me with it.

Sitting down upon the bed, I opened the box and placed it in front of me savoring every tiny detail.

Before I knew it, I heard the front door open and Kate's voice call out to me, instantly followed by footsteps coming up the stairs and, in a panic, I grabbed the box from off the bed, wincing as a sharp pain spread through the palm of my hand.

I didn't have time to look to see what was causing the pain, knowing that at any moment Kate would walk through the door and catch me with her present, ruining her Christmas surprise.

Cursing, I ducked down and thrust it back under the bed just as she walked through the door.

"Dylan are you okay?" she asked, her expression one of confusion and concern. "I've been trying to ring you for hours."

"Hours? you only just left for work," I replied, then blinked in shock as I suddenly realised daylight had started to turn to dusk outside the window. Seeing that I was starting to worry her, I told Kate that I had felt a migraine coming on shortly after she had left for work and decided to go for a lay down and must have slept the day away without realizing, before patting the mattress beside me and gesturing her over to join me.

"Don't get any ideas" she grinned as she sat beside me and laying her head upon my shoulder.

"Me? Never," I grinned. "I can't believe it's Christmas in a few days."

Kate let out a little sigh at my words, I could tell she thought that I had forgotten our anniversary, not that I ever would, after all, I had married the woman of my dreams on Christmas day.

How can anyone forget something like that?

"I'm going for a shower and no before you ask you can't join me," she teased, standing up and making her way to the bathroom door, undressing and dropping her work clothes as she went. She always left a trail of clothing where ever she undressed, and it was the only thing that really irritated me about her.

I was the neat freak in our relationship, and she just left every room looking like a tornado had just passed through. Collecting the clothes off the floor, I tossed them into the wash hamper and made my way downstairs, my thoughts drifting back to the box.

A sharp burning sensation in the palm of my left hand grabbed my attention, and I glanced down to discover that in my haste to shove the box back under the bed I had apparently cut myself on a bed spring.

It was only a small, ragged scratch yet it was deep enough to draw blood and hurt enough to notice.

There was something familiar about it, almost as if I was experiencing DeJa'Vu yet I couldn't explain it.

Pushing the feeling to the back of my mind for the moment, I headed through to the kitchen to cook.

A few hours later I gave Kate a goodnight kiss, wished her sweet dreams and took myself off to bed for the night. I crawled in to bed, slipping beneath the cool sheets, and the moment my head hit the pillow I must have fallen asleep. The next thing I knew I woke in the darkness to Kate's hands slowly making their way up my legs again just like the previous evening.

I didn't want her to stop, I tried to stifle a gasp of ecstasy to no avail. As her hands slid further up, I felt my body start to quiver, she must have felt this too as the pressure of her touch suddenly got heavier, almost as if she wanted me to stop moving, her nails scraped at my skin and before I knew it, I could feel her lips upon my skin. I reached down and stroked her hair as she slowly kissed her way up my inner thigh, I groaned again, my body shifting under her touch.

Three

"Dylan?" Kate's voice called from the bedroom doorway as she turned the light switch on, illuminating our bedroom, genuine concern in her voice.

"WHAT THE FUCK… how…what...who?" I stuttered in a panic, my mind frantically trying to make sense of how Kate had just been with me on the bed but was now somehow standing in the doorway.

Damn, it had been nothing but a dream.

A very vivid dream but a dream, nonetheless.

I managed to calm myself enough to pay attention to Kate who had now crawled into bed beside me, chuckling as she snuggled in against my naked body. "Dreaming of someone special?"

"Always," I replied, running my hand slowly up and down the center of her back, hoping to entice her to a bit of late-night fun but she was clearly overtired.

Within a few minutes the usual whistling and grunting from Kate told me she had fallen asleep, and I found myself lying in the darkness, alone with my own thoughts once again. My mind drifting off to the cherrywood box tucked safely underneath the bed.

The next morning, I woke and headed straight through to our bathroom, knowing that I needed a shower after last night while Kate was sound asleep.

Turning on the shower dial, I checked the water temperature before jumping in, the shower was always hit and miss to get the correct temperature either running too cold or too hot, but this was perfect.

The bathroom had started to steam up as I stepped in the shower and pulled the frosted glass door closed, the hot water hitting my face was so refreshing. For several moments, I just stood beneath the rushing water, enjoying its caress before beginning to lather soap onto my skin then sudden movement at the shower door caught my attention.

Turning, I watched as Kate's naked form moved into the light of the room, the steam fogged up the glass teasing at the beauty of her curves and figure.

"You joining me?" I called out over the water, hoping that she would, it had been a few months since we last had a bit of fun in the shower and I hoped that since we were two days away from our anniversary, she would be feeling a little adventurous once again.

She didn't speak but I watched as she seductively made her way closer to the glass, her breasts bouncing as she walked towards the door, mesmerizing me.

As she reached level with the glass, the bathroom door opened behind her, and I heard the voice of Kate speaking to me as she entered.

I froze in fear, my mind trying to make sense of what was happening before I realized the figure, I had just seen at the shower door was not there. Heart hammering in my chest, I slid the door open and stared out at my wife, unable to form a sentence.

"Are you okay Dylan, you look like you've just seen a ghost," she chuckled as she stepped toward the towel I had left hanging on the radiator. I tried to speak but couldn't find the words, my mind struggling to make sense of what had just happened.

The only rational explanation I could think of was that I had fallen asleep for a second in the shower and had dreamed it all again. Was that even possible?

"Can you pass me the towel" I asked, still trying to make sense of what happened moments before.

She did as I asked, and I began to dry myself as I addressed her. "I think I'm going crazy Kate; I keep seeing things that aren't there."

"What are you talking about Dylan?" she asked, her voice filled with concern. "Talk to mem babe."

"I just saw you walking toward the shower naked, teasing me" I replied, eyes studying her face.

"Oh, you're not going crazy that was me," she replied, the amusement in her voice. "I thought it would be funny to frighten you. Sorry."

She giggled as she stepped closer to the shower door, but something about the noise and the way she moved made me feel uneasy, and I watched as she slowly started to remove her clothes, hesitating on each button of the nightshirt that she was wearing. I couldn't shake the feeling something wasn't right.

As she finally undid the last button of her shirt, she shrugged the shirt off her shoulders and let it drop to the floor, her pale skin seemed to almost glow under the florescent light. I stepped back from the shower door and gestured for her to come in, wanting nothing more than to take her in my arms, my ill feelings pushed away by my growing arousal, but as I reached out for her hand, she stepped back toward the sink, turning and picking up a razor from the cabinet.

I tried to speak but no sound left me and I watched in confusion as she grasped the plastic casing the razor head was housed in, pulling it apart before removing the small blade and raising it to her chest.

Watching in horror, unable to speak, I stared in disbelief as she slowly dragged the razor across her chest, drawing blood as her skin split under the blade.

My body would not move, no matter how hard I tried; no sound left my lips when I tried to scream at her to stop. Instead, I just stood frozen on the spot, forced to watch as my beautiful wife took the razor once again and began to slice at her left nipple. The rose-pink flesh stretched beneath her fingers as she pulled with her free hand, somehow moaning in ecstasy as the small nub of flesh slid free from her.

"Are you enjoying the show?" she grinned at me as she slowly raised the razor blade to her mouth.

Why couldn't I move, why was I being forced to witness my beautiful wife harming herself?

I tried to scream but still no sound left my mouth, and I was forced to watch as Kate licked her lips seductively before slowly putting the blade to the tip of her tongue. I felt my stomach lurch, and then the blade was carving deep into the wet muscle, as she slowly licked its length, splitting her tongue in two.

"Enough fun for me, now it's your turn," she snarled, her teeth stained red, blood dripping from her mouth. My body remained frozen, no matter what I tried I couldn't move or scream, my eyes pleaded with her to stop but she either didn't notice or didn't care.

With her free hand, Kate grabbed me by my wet hair and with unnatural strength yanked my head down toward the razor clasped in her other hand. I hissed in pain as a sharp burning sensation spread through me as she slowly slid the steel blade across my forehead and down my left cheek.

My blood was running freely, hot on the flesh of my naked body as I tried to free myself from her grasp, but she held me with embarrassing ease. I tensed in shock as her fingers slid under the incisions that she had just made either side of my eyes.

Tears were the only release my body could manage to express the excruciating agony that I was experiencing, and before I knew it the room was starting to fade as my vision turned black and I felt the weight of my body disappear.

FOUR

I awoke on the bed, soaking wet with sweat, to find Kate looming over me with a concerned expression upon her face. "Jesus Christ, Dylan, you must have been having some seriously fucked up dream."

"A dream?" I muttered reaching out to touch her face, hoping to dear god that's all it was. My heart was still hammering in my chest, I rolled over and looked at the time on my phone. It was three in the morning.

"Are you OK?"

"You tried to skin my face!" I gasped, still remembering the unbearable pain and the feeling of her fingers sliding under my skin, the wet noise and the excruciating hot pain as my skin was slowly peeled from the tissue connecting it to my skull, still with me.

"Why would I skin your face?" she chuckled, bending down to give me a kiss on the forehead.

It felt so real, but I guess that explained why I couldn't move or even scream or speak.

Sleep paralysis would explain it.

Yet no matter what I could not shake the feeling it was more than just a dream.

I gave Kate a kiss on the cheek and tried to settle back down to sleep but the image of her peeling the flesh from my face kept flashing before my eyes.

My skin prickled with an almost electric feeling and a metallic taste filled my mouth, and I felt a wave of nausea wash over me. Clapping a hand to my mouth, I jumped out of bed and rushed toward the bathroom as the contents of my stomach raced up my throat and tried to vacate my body only to be stopped as it hit the back of my gritted teeth.

Somehow, against the odds, I made it and bent over the sink as I emptied the acrid chunks from my mouth before turning the tap on to wash it down my stomach turning as bits of bile stuck in the plughole. Kate must have followed me to the bathroom as I turned to find her watching me from the open doorway, a towel held in one hand. "Dylan?"

"I'm sorry I didn't mean to wake you again," I told her, grabbing the towel and wiping my mouth. She chuckled, waving a hand as she turned toward the bedroom, shuffling her way sleepily back to bed.

I wanted so much to follow her and get back to bed, to just fall asleep and to wake up the next morning to put this awful night behind me, but I couldn't bring myself to go back to the bedroom.

Instead, I headed down the stairs to the way to the kitchen and made a coffee before sitting down at the counter. For what felt like an eternity, I sat in silence, staring at nothing, my thoughts lingering upon the awful nightmare that had awoken me earlier.

I must have fallen asleep as one moment I was sat with a hot steaming mug of coffee in front of me and in the blink of an eye it was daylight, and my coffee was now stone cold and untouched.

"Morning sleepy head, do you want a fresh cup of coffee?" Kate grinned from across the counter, surprising me with her presence. "I came down and you were asleep sitting up in the chair, eyes wide open. You literally scared the shit out of me at first as you were just sat staring into space."

"Sorry I couldn't sleep so I came down so you could get some rest, I must have nodded off," I replied, pushing the cold cup mug to one side. "It's weird I've been having some really strange dreams the past few nights."

I felt like I was slowly losing my mind; I had lost time and my dreams felt like real experiences.

But then I was under a lot of pressure with work, and I guess it was finally all starting to affect me.

"You've probably been working too hard, one more day and we will both be on Christmas break, it's almost time to party" Kate said as she did a silly dance on the spot. "It's Christmas time baby!"

I grinned as I made my way around the counter and wrapped my arms around Kate's waist, giving her a kiss on the side of the cheek "I love you."

"I love you too, but I'm going to be late for work," she said, as she glanced at her phone and stepped away from me. "I have to go!"

"Sure," I gave her a sly pat on the arse as she walked past me and followed her down the hall, heading into my office to get myself started with my last day of work. Working from home was more of a curse than it was a blessing, as I found my mind running off track again and drifting back towards the box under the bed once more.

FIVE

I switched on my computer and threw myself in to work until lunch time, promising myself if I stayed focused and worked until it was time to eat that I would allow myself a small break to go upstairs and check on the box. I had to make sure it was still safe upstairs under the bed.

Lunch time arrived and I made my way upstairs. Upon entering the bedroom, I rushed to the side.

of the bed the box was hidden under and reached to grab it, only to find it missing. Panic spread over me that the surprise was ruined, and Kate had already somehow found it. I dropped to the floor, throwing the sheets up and peering under but nothing. I got back up and walked around to Kate's side of the bed and just as I was about to check the bedside cabinet, I had a sudden memory of taking the box in to the bathroom the night before to clean it after I had noticed I had gotten a bit of blood on it from the cut on my hand. I blinked and gave my head a shake. The memory felt real but at the same time it felt false, like the hangover from a dream.

There was only one way to be sure.

Barging in the bathroom, I knocked the laundry hamper over as the door caught it, and as the basket hit the floor, the towels toppled out revealing the box.

Grabbing it up out of the pile of dirty towels, I made my way back downstairs to my office and placed the box on the desk beside my computer. I had a few hours before Kate would be home and then I just needed to keep it hidden one more night.

I threw myself back in to work for a few more hours and then set about wrapping the box up and placing it under the tree in the living room before heading into the kitchen and starting the dinner.

I heard the front door open and close and moments later Kate appeared in the kitchen. I had just finished the dinner and was setting the table when a loud pop from the living room startled me and caused me to drop the glass I was holding, which shattered across the tiled floor. A second later the lights went out and we were cast in darkness.

"I think a fuse has blown," Kate said as she fumbled to get her phone out of her pocket and swiped at the screen until the flashlight came on, illuminating her pretty features and I let out a terror induced scream as a face loomed out of the darkness behind her, before disappearing in the blink of an eye.

"Dylan! What's wrong" Kate asked in fear.

For a moment I paused as I tried to make sense of what just happened, I mean how do you explain to someone you just saw their face staring at you from over their own shoulder. Except the face wasn't the thing of beauty that Kate wore now, but a mask of horror. Its features disfigured, the skin twisted and contorted, with a look of decay about it.

"I stepped on a bit of glass," I told her, trying to sound as truthful as possible as I didn't want to worry her. After all, the dreams I had been having had obviously been messing with my head.

"I think the fuse has tripped; I'll go reset it," I told her making my way through the darkness of the kitchen as Kate used the light from her phone to clean the broken glass.

The streetlight outside cast a fraction of light through the glass of the front door, illuminating a small fraction of the hallway just beside the fuse box allowing me to see that the main fuse had indeed been tripped. Flicking the switch, I watched as the lights all came back on and then jumped backward in shock as the passageway light bulb exploded above me, casting a shower of glass over the floor and myself.

In that split second flash of light, I could have sworn I caught a glimpse of a woman standing just off to the side of the stairs, her long brown hair covering her features so I couldn't quite make out who she was.

Something about her felt familiar, but the moment my eyes readjusted she had gone once more and, in her place, I found the coat rack, the long brown scarf hanging from the top hook and Kate's peach coloured long woolen coat having caused the illusion.

Maybe that's why she had felt so familiar.

I made my way back through to the kitchen and grabbed the dustpan and brush, then went back and cleaned the mess in the hallway up, glancing over my shoulder toward the tree in the living room where Kate's present lay wrapped as I did.

I couldn't wait to see her face when I presented her with something that I knew she would love.

I found myself picturing the next morning, Kate sat patiently, her eyes closed as she awaited her present, me handing her the parcel and watching with glee as she unwrapped the box, her features split with trepidation and excitement as she studied it.

In my mind's eye, I waited for the smile which never came, instead her mouth opened as if to speak but the sound that left her was not human but rather the loud, soulless clicking of an insect. Her neck began to bulge and the muscles beneath began to palpitate. I sat watching in horror as the sound escaping her open mouth grew louder, the call of demonic cicadas, a cacophony of terror, and then Kate lunged forward, evacuating the contents of her esophagus onto the seat. Hundreds of tiny little black beetles fell from her mouth, dropping onto the sofa and floor before she suddenly snapped her head backward and let out a blood curdling scream. As I stood staring down in terror, the beetles started surrounding my feet, their tiny little pincers lancing into the tips of my toes and as I kicked out to try and shake them free, I snapped myself out of the daydream and gave a shaky breath.

SIX

On trembling legs, I headed back into the kitchen, trying to push the last few minutes behind me and enjoy Christmas Eve with my beautiful wife.

When we finished our meal and headed upstairs, I ran Kate a bath and then headed off to bed to await her.

I knew Kate would be a while, so I decided to relax and watch some tv, and flicking through the channels I settled for an old re-run of quantum leap and within moments I felt my eyes closing. The past few days had worn me out and as much as I tried to stay awake for Kate's return, my body and fatigue were winning.

I awoke a few hours later to find Kate sitting at the bottom of the bed still wrapped in her towel, her eyes staring back at me coldly.

"Are you okay," I asked as I crawled down the bed, reaching out a hand to gently caress her shoulders. "DON'T touch me!" she snapped. "I don't know how you dare touch me after what you did!"

"What?" I asked, getting off the bed to walk round to see her face. "What do you mean? Kate please, I don't know what you're talking about."

"You did this to me" she said as she turned to face me, her skin grey and mottled, a hand pulling the towel from her body as she stood, dropping it to the floor, to reveal a large bloody void in her chest. "You stole my heart!"

I stepped back quickly as I gasped in shock, the back of my legs colliding heavily with the chest of drawers. I fell off balance, hitting my head on the mirror, causing my vision to turn black momentarily.

Blinking hard as my sight returned to normal, I found that Kate was nowhere to be seen, and the towel she had dropped was gone from the floor.

I rushed toward the bathroom, calling her name, and threw the door open, gasping in relief as Kate let out a little shriek of terror at my sudden bursting into the bathroom.

"I'm so sorry I didn't mean to frighten you," I said bending forward and giving her a kiss. "I had another bad dream…an awful dream, and I wanted to make sure you where okay."

"You want to join me, more like," she winked, sliding back up the tub to make room for me, and despite my dread of moments before, she didn't need to ask me twice. A few moments later I was in the tub with her, and we were recreating our wedding night.

After our fun in the tub, we headed to bed and fell asleep in each other's arms, content and safe.

The next morning, Christmas morning, I awoke to find Kate that had already gotten up. I could hear her singing along to Christmas carols in the kitchen below and I rushed down the stairs to see her.

"Good morning my beautiful wife," she said as I walked through the kitchen door, her eyes sparkling as she met my gaze. "I've made you a coffee and some breakfast babe...and happy anniversary."

"Five years together and I'm still falling more in love with you every day" I told her.

"I can't wait to make it another five years."

We sat and ate our breakfast before heading into the living room together for the gift exchange.

Despite my age, I was as excited as a kid and couldn't wait for her to see her special gift. As she got comfortable on the sofa, I grabbed the box out from under the tree and handed her the present.

SEVEN

Bottom lip caught between my teeth, I watched with anticipation as she slowly but carefully removed each piece of tape holding the wrapping paper down. She knew how to keep me in suspense, and this was killing me. Finally, she started to unwrap the paper and remove the box from within. I watched with bated breath, waiting for her reaction, my mind in overdrive.

Did she love it, hate it.

I needed to know.

"I absolutely love it" she said as she studied the box, her hand slowly caressing the engraving of the two turtle doves, tears in her eyes. "Where did you manage to find it, it's exactly the same as the one my grandmother had as a child."

She leaned forward, kissing me gently on the lips.

"I knew the minute I spotted it in the antique shop down the road that you would love it," I told her as I moved closer to her, a faraway look in her eyes.

She sat for a moment studying the box, turning it over and over, before running her hand over the turtle doves again, her brow furrowed. Then she gave a soft grunt of triumph as she pushed her fingers hard on the beak of one of the birds, and I watched in amazement as she slowly pulled the two birds apart, revealing a hidden compartment between the pair.

Upon opening the compartment, a foul odor emanated from within, making us both gag, our eyes streaming with tears as we over-coughed. Reaching inside, she pulled out an object wrapped in a deep red cloth, I had no idea what it was or that the box even opened, and as I sat transfixed watching, as Kate slowly started unwrapping the object, the smell grew worse as the cloth was removed. and for a moment, we both sat unsure of what it was she was holding.

Then I remembered.

The tears stung my eyes and ran down my cheeks as I could no longer deny the truth, memories of the past few days flooding back to me. Replaying in my mind, I watched myself make my way across the bathroom, reaching the sink and picking up the razor resting on its side. Kate was standing in the shower watching me as I fumbled at the plastic, the blade slicing my palm as it slipped free from its casing.

I drew the blade across my chest and then slowly hacked at my nipple, before cutting it free and putting the flesh in my mouth. I wanted the memories to stop, but they kept coming. In my memories, I made my way over to Kate who stood frozen in horror in the open door of the shower, frozen in terror as I slowly dragged the razor across her beautiful face, before sliding my fingers into the cuts, the supple flesh giving way as I peeled the skin back, revealing raw muscle and bone beneath. She passed out at this point, cracking her head off the side of the tub as she slipped down, causing the water to run red as the blood from her now faceless skull mixed with that from the shower head. Holding her face in my hands I walked over to the mirror, and placed it upon my own, smoothing the skin over my features before brushing my matted brown hair back out of the way so I could admire my new mask.

I closed my eyes trying to block the memories, but they kept coming. This time I was forced to relive the moment I removed her heart and put it in the box.

I watched as I made my way to the kitchen, grabbed a meat cleaver from the knife rack and made my way back to the bathtub. Christmas carols where playing in the background. Suddenly I was in the bathroom, meat cleaver raised above my head, the intense rage I felt that day washed back over me. She was going to leave me for her workmate. She had told me she had been having an affair for the past year and a half and in her heart, she knew it was time to put an end to our marriage. She tore my heart out that day, so I tore hers out. I brought the cleaver down hard on her chest, the blade cutting deep into her breast, the flesh parting as the wet slop of blood sprayed the ceiling and walls as I raised the cleaver again before quickly bringing it down over and over until there was nothing but a bloody pulp where her breast had once been, her ribs, nothing more than jagged bone. I slipped my hand into the pulpy mess, wrapping my hand around the warm muscle and yanked hard. Nothing. I tried again and again until eventually with a wet squelching sound it gave way and pulled free. I wrapped it up and placed it inside the box then hid it under the bed before taking her downstairs. I propped her up on the sofa and removed her face from mine, placing it back on her skull haphazardly. I left her there sat in front of the Christmas tree with her favorite Christmas song on repeat.

Everything I had experienced the past few days now made sense; my brain had been trying to make me face the truth as my mind had fragmented into some fairytale Happy ending to hide the true horror I had carried out and I let out a chuckle as George Micheals Voice sang from the Alexa. "Last Christmas I gave you, my heart."

Three French Hens
Megan Stockton

Eloise always thought that the ultimate betrayal was when a place that should have been heaven on earth turned into hell. She still remembered the first time that they stepped foot in the adorable little farmhouse on the outskirts of the city. Her mother had beamed with joy, and she had thought this would be the fresh start they all had needed. She thought that it may change her husband, that somehow this little home possessed a sort of magic that could have cored out the rotten parts of him. Eloise and her sisters may not have believed it was possible but, damned if they didn't *hope*…

But their mother died screaming. They said she may have had an aneurysm, something that caused her sudden and painful death. The girls knew better. They heard her wails through the thin walls: her begging and pleading and apologies.

Some nights, like tonight, Eloise thought that she could still hear those sounds distant and muffled like they were trapped in the bones of the house. She rolled carefully, tucked tight between her two older sisters in the small bed, trying not to wake them. Her older sister Margot immediately woke, eyes snapping open as though she had never been truly asleep to start with. She propped herself up onto an elbow, large eyes a pool of chocolatey calmness in the dim night. The mattress sagged in the larger girl's direction, and Eloise rolled into her soft form.

"What is it?" Margot asked quietly.

"Sometimes I think I hear mother. In the walls, in the floors."

Margot's lips pursed together in a thin line, and she shook her head, reaching up to tap her knuckles on Eloise's forehead, "Not in the walls, not in the floors... Just in here. Sometimes our minds are the enemy, you know. Our own personal prisons."

Eloise snuggled into her big sister and fell asleep.

Noel Dubois sat at the head of their small table, reading a rain-damp copy of the local paper. The moisture had made the thin paper nearly transparent, words bleeding from the opposite side and making it nearly illegible. It irritated him, and cursed in his native tongue as he used his calloused fingertips to turn the pages in frustration.

Eloise was sitting quietly at the table as she finished school work. Margot was cleaning off the countertops with a determined fury. Their youngest sister, Bijou, was reaching into a wire basket to retrieve the last egg. She clutched it between her fingers as she stepped off the small stool and strode past the table to the stove where a pat of butter was melting patiently in a warmed pan. The content humming in her throat diminished as she passed behind Eloise, and she heard the sound of something hitting the floor with a faint *crack*.

Even before Eloise turned, she knew that Bijou had dropped the egg. Not just an egg though, it was the last egg that they had. Noel had traded someone down the road for a dozen of them, as money had been so tight recently. He had a single egg for breakfast every morning. *Every morning.* Eloise slowly looked over her shoulder. As though she was seeing everything in slow motion, she looked down at the cracked brown shell and the contents of the egg spilled on the floor. The yolk, still intact, scooted across the tile like a ship across a smooth ocean. Eloise's doe-eyes were brimmed with surprised tears, hand pressed to her painted lips. Her hair was in tight columns of curls, and they bounced lightly around her face as she leaned down to clean it up. She always got ready like this, every day. She got all dolled up for nobody, she loved to feel pretty. She was beautiful and pure and gentle.

There was a brief moment of silence and calm, and then everything exploded.

Noel stood so quickly that his chair toppled over behind him. He rushed towards Bijou with his hand raised above his head, palm outstretched. From the other side of the room Margot was also on the move. Eloise didn't know how she did it, but in an instant, she was between their little sister and their father. She put her arms back, defending the younger girl with her own body. She snarled at her father; thick brows pulled down over her dark eyes. She went from a beautiful young woman to a feral creature that would tear your throat out.

Noel hit her.

Eloise not only saw and heard it, but she felt it. When his palm struck her across the cheek and forehead, she thought she could feel it in her own chest. Margot stumbled backwards and would have fallen if not for Bijou grappling to support her larger frame. Her head snapped back, but she quickly righted herself, stumbling forward. She was unsteady, but she stood onto her own feet, hands twisted into fists as she stared up at him. He stared back and raised his hand as though he'd hit her again.

"No!" Bijou squealed, tears streaming down her face.

Noel's chest heaved and he hissed between his teeth, spittle flying at the two girls, before he stomped across the room and out the front door, slamming it behind him.

"Margot…" Eloise whispered, finally able to move from her frozen place at the table. The fear that had her immobilized melted away and she was covered in a white-hot despair. She rushed over to the eldest Dubois girl and helped her settle onto the floor. The three of them huddled together as they examined and tried to tend to Margot's rapidly swelling face: eye nearly obscured by the tissue that was growing fatter and blacker by the second.

Margot let them fuss over her for a few moments and then she stood up, smoothing her oversized T-shirt as though it were a gown. As dressed up as Bijou always was, Margot was always dressed down. She smiled at the two of them and touched just her middle finger to her swollen eye.

"This has to stop," Bijou whispered.

Eloise looked over at her and shook her head, "Get a towel and clean up this egg, Bijou. Maybe if it's cleaned up before he gets home, he will forget about it…"

"Even if he does," she argued, "it will just be something else. You can't keep protecting us, Margot. You're going to end up just like…"

Margot shot her a look, gaze venomous and sharp. Bijou shrunk into herself, chin falling down and hair obscuring her eyes.

"She's not wrong." Eloise agreed quietly. She surprised herself, voice startling her so much that she closed her jaw with an audible click. But she already had Margot's attention.

"So, you think so too?" Margot asked. "Both of you? You think we could survive without him?"

"This isn't living either, Margot." Bijou then mused: "But he *is* our father, and we have nowhere to go. If we can just survive a few more years… I've been trying to find a nice boy, someone who in a few years might…"

Margot scoffed, "Out of the frying pan and into the fire. You really want to get out from under the thumb of one man, and run right underneath another?"

Bijou's brows furrowed, scolding her sister with her gaze, "Margot, not all men…"

"Not all women are pushovers either. Did you know that we own this house? Outright, I mean. So, let's kill him."

All color drained from Bijou's face, and Eloise felt both the warmth and blood fade from hers as well.

"*Kill* him? *Kill him?* No one said anything about killing anybody, Margot. I thought more along the lines of running away or calling the police or…"

"I have something I want to show you. Both of you. Tonight, after he's home and watching television, I want you to meet me in the cellar."

Eloise hoped that Bijou would ask Margot what she had to show them, but she did not inquire. The rest of the day dragged on, excruciating minute by minute. Eloise waited for an opportunity to talk to Margot alone. She thought that maybe if they could discuss things, it would alleviate this creeping sensation of dread that was building in her gut. She thought all of the house's dark corners had faces, that she could hear whispering voices in the drains and pipes of the old home. She thought that she could feel cool hands on the back of her neck as she passed the door to the downstairs. She thought that Margot possessed a too-large shadow that lengthened and grew as the day died.

The time finally came, as the last golden fingertips of the sun clutched to the horizon. Their father collapsed into his worn and weathered recliner: its arms matted flat with the oils and grease from his body and clothes throughout the year. It was a dull but shiny black and carried with it a mildly foul odor. He became a series of mountains and valleys in the dark, form only visible from the blue light of the television as it flashed in the room.

Eloise noticed that the door to the cellar was open, a gaping maw of inky black that seemed to reach out with grasping hands. She could hear Margot moving around down there but could not see any movement. She waited at the edge of the kitchen, just barely able to see into the living room. Bijou carried the aluminum tray to her father with a modest dinner on it. She sat it on his stomach and smiled before she hesitantly kissed his forehead.

"Love you," she whispered, but he didn't respond. Instead, he leaned around to see what he was missing on the screen. Something about a sponge: a sponge worth an entire commercial slot.

Bijou walked past Eloise without making eye contact and disappeared into the darkness. Eloise followed her down, each creaking step dropping a degree in the ambient temperature. There was a yellow light bulb glowing in a far corner, somehow obscured from above with the thick dark.

Margot was sitting on the floor with her legs crossed, a wooden plank on the floor in front of her. Bijou seated herself timidly across, tucking her knees up around her chest and hugging them. Eloise found herself rooted to the floor, once more in a state of immobility.

"Margot?" Eloise breathed. "What is that?"

Margot ran her polished fingernails across the top, nails popping against every engraved letter and number, "A spirit board."

It felt ominous. Eloise could never have explained it: the way that it made her feel. It had a tugging, a pull, like something between them wanted to close the space. Something she couldn't see, but that she could feel deep in her chest.

"Margot, I don't like this." Eloise insisted.

Bijou chimed in quietly, voice nearly lost in the heaviness of the air: "What does it do?"

Margot ignored Eloise entirely, instead speaking to Bijou like one might a young child: "I've been talking to someone… Someone who used to live in this house. They can help us with our… problem."

"How?" Bijou asked.

"No, no, no." Eloise said, heart lurching in her chest. "Please, Margot. Something about this doesn't feel right."

"Just put your hand here on the planchette with me, Bij." Margot said, taking her sister's small hands and placing them on the heart-shaped disk in the middle of the board.

"Please, Margot. Let's take just a minute to talk about this." Eloise begged, putting her hands out. She felt like she was talking someone off of a ledge, trying to get them to just step down and reconsider that long jump down.

She didn't hear her sisters as they started speaking, asking questions, extending invitations. She only knew that she felt the cold arms of something wrap around her. It was a gentle squeeze, something that was almost comforting. She found herself nuzzling her nose into it, a drowsiness overcoming her and making her skull feel heavy.

"Margot? Bijou?" she asked groggily. She realized her eyes were closed in a long, sleepy blink and she forced them open. Everything was hazy and slow, passing by and leaving copies of itself behind. She could see her sisters standing now, hands clamped over their mouths as they stared at her. Bijou's eyes were welled with tears, pregnant drops spilling down her powdered cheeks. Margot, always the strongest of them, stood straight and tall, shoulder protectively covering part of Bijou's body.

But the fear. It was there.

Eloise turned and ascended the stairs, driven by a compulsion that she could only associate with thirst or hunger. An urge of survival that was primitive and unyielding. She found herself groaning in agony, finger tips clawing at her own throat and chest and stomach. Somewhere there resided a deep itch that she just couldn't get to.

She could hear Margot and Bijou calling her name, their voices were shrill and echoing with desperation. They sounded so far away, and her name sounded foreign on their tongues. She jerked open the refrigerator, pulling out a half gallon of milk and unscrewing the lid before she poured it into her mouth so generously that it soaked her. It felt warm, nearly the temperature of something cooked, against her skin and throat.

She became furious and she couldn't explain it. It didn't satisfy her *needs.* She removed a knife from the block on the counter and looked down into its shining surface. Everything clicked. It made sense. What she had to do, needed to do, was very clear. Even as she saw someone else reflected there, no longer her own face. No longer the face of a young girl, but the warped and damaged face of an elderly man. She looked down, seeing her own familiar body and her feminine form. Breasts clawed from her scratching, pouring blood down her shirt and across her thighs.

Eloise's feet, borrowed and driven by someone else, took her to the living room where her father watched television. At the sight of her shadow across the floor, too large, he turned to look at her. She could tell by the look in his eyes that he saw her and not the man that possessed her. His eyes were angry, furious that she had interrupted him.

"What the hell do you think you're doing, girl?" he asked, slamming the foot rest of the recliner down.

Normally the sound would have made Eloise flinch, but she wasn't in control anymore... and she didn't really care. She found herself goading, pulling against a spiritual harness like an eager workhorse. She could not rush her father fast enough. She came to the end table and lifted the metal tray, striking him across the face so hard that the aluminum dented in the middle.

Teeth flew out of Noel's mouth, one leaving a splatter of blood across the television as he bounced off the screen and clattered to the floor. His nose had broken and poured blood. He gurgled and spat, struggling to get to his feet. He stumbled towards her, swinging his fist. She sidestepped to avoid him, and as he tumbled forward, she met him with the knife, burying it into his guts.

The cold milk had felt warm, but the blood from his bowels as they spilled across her hands like thick rolls of moist fabric felt like fire. She was emboldened and stimulated by the heat of his lifeblood, tearing out his organs like tissue from a gift bag, spilling them into the floor. They were lacerated and bulging with stomach contents both partially, fully, and not-at-all digested. His bladder burst like a soured balloon.

He crumpled to the floor in front of him and Eloise dropped to her knees, rubbing the blood across her erect nipples, up her throat and across her cheeks. It felt so good: an ecstasy she had never felt before. She found her tongue roaming over her own fingertips and then across the knife's blade. She had split her tongue into four or five pieces, chunks falling between her lips and onto her lap but there was no pain. No pain still when she used the tip of the knife to start digging at the roots of her teeth, wiggling them loose and laying them in a line on the floor.

Anything to stop the itching, the deep and unreachable irritation.

"Eloise!"

She heard someone scream her name again, but she was so absorbed in the task at hand (every tooth, pull every one of them out until the itching stopped) that she didn't recognize who it may have been.

Someone put hands on her and she pulled away. They tugged at her clothing, and came to sit between her, trying to pull the knife out of her hands and away from her mouth.

"Eloise, please stop."

She couldn't stop, and no one would stop her. She turned the knife around and plunged it into Margot's eye. She followed through, pushing far beyond her eye and into the back of her skull. Eloise buried that knife to the hilt, waiting until it clicked against the orbital sockets. Jelly oozed around the blade, but it bled so little. She felt so unsatisfied. Margot began reciting children's poems, voice jerky and unnatural. It wasn't her anymore. Not unlike the possession that Eloise was dealing with, someone had grabbed the wheel inside Margot and tried to steer the vehicle back onto the road as she sat dead at the wheel. She screamed the lyrics to "Il était un petit navire" between gasping breaths as she fell to the floor.

It was Bijou's voice that Eloise heard next. She knew the small, innocent voice. Eloise put her bare feet against Margot's paddling body, pulling the knife from her eye and watching as Margot's hands began to flutter at the end of her wrists with every tug.

Bijou called for her again, but it was too late. Eloise found herself splitting open her own stomach, watching as her tissue spread at the pressing of the blade like a perfectly risen dough: layer by layer. She closed her eyes as she buried her hands into the heat there: the fires of Hell were in their bowels this entire time. She relished the heat.

Another scream from Bijou's lungs. She was begging, sobbing. Things were changing around Eloise, very slowly. Everything was made of stretchy rubber, and someone was pulling it away. It shivered and warped, smearing and swirling and finally coming to rest in stillness. She could suddenly smell blood and piss and shit, and she felt so cold and sticky. The heat was gone.

Then the pain came. Everywhere. All at once.

Four Calling Birds

Angel Van Atta

It was Christmas morning when the four birds came a calling. The first was a beautiful and fragile thing. Its tiny, frail bones were hidden beneath a fluff of white feathers with splashes of brown all mixed through. Its little black eyes, small fierce dots peeking out at me, and I knew it was beckoning me. Demanding that I follow. There was something about those eyes, something that made it impossible not to obey.

The cacophony of the world behind me lessened as I walked toward the tiny creature as it fluttered wildly about, zipping through the air ahead in a frenzied triangle of flapping wings, and all the while, its little gaze held mine. Part of me wanted to look back, to see what all the shouting was about, but I couldn't. I was helpless to it. I was lost to it.

So, I followed. I followed, and it fluttered away, and away I went, trying my best to keep up, but my body felt weird, different somehow in a way I couldn't quite grasp. I felt lighter than normal, detached.

As my feet crunched on through the light dusting of snow that had fallen since I had first seen the bird there before me, a thick fog rolled in. It was dampening the sounds of the people who had begun to run back the way I had come, toward whatever it was the bird was calling me away from. With the sound also went the sight of the buildings to my left and the street to my right. But I hardly noticed these things as I tried my best to keep up, for all I could do was think about where it was leading me. I had no cares left about what was behind me now. That was for some other me in some other when. Now, all that mattered was the bird and not losing sight of it as the fog rolled in.

On and on we went, and soon, there was no sound at all and no sights from the world around me; the mist was so thick. I knew the air was cold because the breath puffed out of me in teeny clouds of white that were almost instantly lost in the mist that filled the world just now. All that was left was me and the little feathered creature madly flying around ahead.

On and on we went, and just as I was beginning to think there was no hope, I would lose the bitty thing in all this white, I noticed something new. Something beautiful but eerie in this dense air. Something that brought back so much joy and so much dread all at once. It was the twinkling of lights.

These lights, though, they weren't new lights, no. These were lights I recognized at once, for they were familiar lights. Lights from long ago in a time I never thought I would see again. A time that had been stolen from me on a Christmas morning, much like this one had been. For those lights were hung in the same exact way that my father had always hung them, and they were the same identical string from all those years ago, I would know them anywhere.

The green lights popped up first and then just after the reds, blues, oranges, and yellows. They came softly at first, just a whisper of shades through the fog, but then there they were, and their pattern left me with no doubts of the house I would see them on when I got close enough. A few steps later, I knew I was right, for there it was, my childhood home. The one we had moved away from the year my father... Well, the year he took his life.

I had known my father wasn't well. Of course, I had. Even at such a young age, I had known. It was in the way he was happier than anyone should ever be one moment and then sadder and angrier the next. The way he tried to shut his thoughts away by drowning them in a bottle every night when he got home from work and the way I would hear him crying in the bathroom when he thought nobody else was home. It was in the way he always said he loved me after screaming at me to shut up and go away so he could have some peace and quiet, and in the way he begged for my forgiveness after I cried into my pillow each time this happened.

But even though I knew he wasn't well, that he wasn't like the other dads who always seemed to be the same, the happy dads were happy, and the quiet dads were quiet, and the angry dads were angry, instead of all those things all mixed up all the time, I was too young to even know that a person could take their own life. That a person could choose to die. And even if I had, what could I have done? I was just a child.

The bird perched upon the letterbox attached to the wood just to the right of the door and looked at me straight on. It made no noise, and I could hear the sound coming from inside. The sound that I had thought I would never hear again, even though I had heard it almost every Christmas season since. The sound that haunted me in the deepest part of the nights around this time of year when everyone else was sleeping aside from me. When everyone else was blissfully unaware of the Ghost of Christmas Past that came to visit only me.

The door was standing there, painted red, as bright as it had been that day. I was helpless not to continue walking forward, and even though I fought the urge with every single part of my being, my hand kept reaching out, out, out, the closer that I came. And as I finally stood upon the bright Christmas mat my mother had laid out each year for as long as I could remember, my hand closed around that knob. A brilliant shock of icy coldness shot up through my pale, gloveless hand and straight into my very core. For I knew what I would see when I walked in. As my hand slowly turned the knob and I began to put pressure against the door and push it in, as I had that day when we had made it back from church, I suddenly found myself as I was back then. Just a little girl stuck in a nightmare.

The door swung slowly in, and the sound the hinges made mixed in with the sound of the creaking rope. A chill ran up my spine, and had I been able, I would have slammed it shut and ran away from there, back toward the growing crowd of people where this cursed bird had taken me from. But instead, I stood there, eyes wide open, to see it all again.

My father's large body hung from a rope he had tied over the balcony railing above, and as it hung, it swung, and as it swung, it made this eerie creaking sound. But that wasn't the part that haunted me in those early morning moments when the sky was still black outside, and there were no other sounds to interrupt the ghost of this memory, which was now replaying itself before me. No. It was not the worst by far.

As I watched, his body jerked and thrashed as his nails dug into the flesh being crushed by the rope around his neck. They scooped and scratched and made red bloody trails through the purpling skin. His eyes bulged out of his sockets, and it seemed that at any second, they would pop right out of his head. The look of panic, fear, and desperation that shone out at me was almost too much to bear a second time. It would have been too much had there been any way around it.

When he saw me standing there, his hands left the scratching at his throat to reach out for me, as if I could help him, as if I were tall enough or strong enough to lift him up so that he could get a breath and have a chance to loosen the rope. But I was just a child. A scrawny little brat who never ate my vegetables when my mother told me to and who spent my time reading books and playing video games. What could I do to help this man who had suddenly changed his mind and wanted the life back that he had decided to throw away? Suddenly, the weight of living another day seemed much lighter than his body did as gravity pulled it toward the floor.

"Gaaaaaalllllllllleeeeerrrrp," my father moaned out at me. I had no idea what that was supposed to mean, but that didn't stop him from making the sound.

Over and over again, the noise came out, and I could hear how badly he needed me to know in the tone it made with the creaking of the rope. And all I could do was stand there and watch. All I could do was let him die. For there was no other choice for me to make. I was just as helpless then as I was now.

His bulging eyes begged, and his tongue shot out and plumped up, and yellowish ooze dripped from between it and his lips and leaked on down his chin. And there was suddenly a smell. A smell of shit and piss, and a stain appeared and grew on the front of his pants. Then, my mother was finally in the door behind me, and her screams filled the air. And as I turned to see her, just as I had back then, the house was gone, and suddenly there was only the mist.

I was so happy that the scene was no longer there. The scene of that Christmas that had torn my life apart and changed it forever more. But the feeling of guilt I carried was suddenly fresh and new and heavier than it had ever been. The shame of knowing that I watched him die when I could have maybe done something to save his life. I just stood there as the broken man I loved so dearly fought to stay alive, yet I did nothing but stand.

The second bird came moments later as if it were giving me time to soak it all in before making its appearance. As if it wanted me to fully feel all the tragedy I could before bringing me on to whatever it had in store. As if it needed me to fully comprehend the guilt I carried and had carried for so long. As if it couldn't come until that task was done.

This second bird was bigger than the first. A bright red bird with a mohawk of brilliant red feathers atop its head. It, too, seemed small and frail, though it was still three times the size, at least, of the first that had found its way into my life not that long ago. This bird fluttered down upon the ground just before my feet and looked up at me with black eyes just as fierce as that first bird's had been.

I wanted to ask it what it wanted, but no words would leave my lips. And so, I did the only thing I could when it hopped up and took flight, threatening to leave me in the fog alone, in this eerie world that seemed so desolate and void of anything but it and I. I followed after.

It was easier to see than the first bird had been, and I was soon caught up. As I walked, I realized that the snow beneath my feet was getting deeper, and the ground beneath the snow was made of hardened dirt and stone and grass. There was a trail of sorts that we were on, and I recognized it, too, all at once, and I knew. I knew what this horrid bird was taking me to see.

I could hear the water rushing by up ahead, and I could hear the shouting of my mother as I went, and suddenly I was running. I needed to get to where I had stood all those years ago. Maybe this time I could help. Maybe this time, I could save her.

But once I was there, I knew there would be no second chance. For this was not me traveling back through time. This was a recounting. A weighing of my crimes through the guilt that bore me down through my life. And this was on a Christmas morning, too.

My mother had taken us to the giant hill to sled. It was a few years after my father had so violently slipped away and she was trying to make Christmas a more special time again. To replace the bad memories with ones much better. But instead, there was only more to lose and more guilt to carry.

Greta and I had pushed the sled up the hill a dozen times at least that day and then ridden it down again. Each time, she had wanted to go higher and higher, and I had wholeheartedly agreed. Her large brown eyes were so happy that day, and our brand-new sled, which we had found under the Christmas tree, was so shiny and red. As red as the feathers of the bird which had brought me here.

Up and up and up, we had climbed over and over again, and each time, we had zoomed down to the bottom where my mother stood between us and the river that rushed by at her back so that she could stop us if she needed to. And each time, she would warn us to go no higher because we were going too fast and too far, and she was worried about the water. Finally, she had had enough of us pressing our luck and had said it was time to go, and I had begged and whined and pleaded for her to let us have just one more chance. One more speedy race down to the bottom on this magical Christmas morning, and finally, she relented.

Greta had not wanted to climb all the way to the top, for she had been tired by this point, but I kept going. It was the last time we would get to ride this new shiny toy for who knew how long, and I loved the way the wind felt against my face as we barreled down the hill. It felt for a moment during that short time that I could outpace the memory of my father dangling there. It felt as if I could outrun his desperate gaze as his eyes bulged out from his lids, and that sound of the creaking rope mixed with those gurgling pleas as he died before me.

"No more, no more," she had begged, and I ignored her words, and she had followed as I knew she would. For I was her big sister, and nothing I could do could ever seem bad to her. Nothing I could do could ever seem dangerous, not really.

Finally, we made it to the top, and my mother's yells for us to not go were mostly lost in the wind, so I felt that I could later claim plausible deniability. Little did I know that there would be no denying my fault in this in my own heart. That this choice would be a burden I would forever have to carry.

Greta climbed aboard, though she was reluctant to, for she could hear our mother's screams as much as I. "Are you sure?" she asked, her voice so low and shaky with the fright she felt, but I ignored that sound because my own excitement to rush down and outrun my guilt was just too large. I wish I would have listened to it. I wish I would have really heard her trepidation. I wish I would have felt it, too.

Instead of answering her, I climbed on and pushed off as hard as I could. I wanted the wind to sting as we flew down the hill, and I wasn't disappointed. Faster and faster and faster, we raced, and for a second, my heart rejoiced because it worked. The only thing there was to feel was wind and speed and rush. The rush filled my heart and mind, and for a second, there was nothing else as the ice-cold snow bit into my cheeks. My knitted red cap flew off my head, allowing my long mouse-brown hair to fly out behind me and whip about. My father's death was far away, and all there was, was this.

"Stop!" My mother screamed as we raced toward her down the hill. "You're going too fast!"

And then reality crashed back in as my mother's figure grew closer and closer, and I realized that we wouldn't be able to stop in time. I could see the edge of the river as it grew behind her. I could hear the rushing sound it made as the water within crashed against the rocks as it raced on by, and I knew that if we went in, it would take me, too. It would be the ultimate race against the guilt of my father's end. It would wrap me up in its cold embrace, and finally, I would find the peace I so desperately wanted. If only I had known that it wouldn't be me who death would accept that day. That it would be my precious little sister who would be taken. If only I had known what weight I would carry from this new day and how heavy it would be upon my heart, and mind, and soul.

My mother tried to catch us, to put herself before us and have us crash into her instead of flying right past into the water's freezing rushing path. But as she jumped and swerved, so too did I. I thought if I jumped off and kicked, the sled would turn sideways and topple us into the snow, but all it did was cause the shiny wooden bottom to coast around my mother as she slammed into the snow and continue on its way toward my sister's sad demise.

"Greta, Jump!" I screeched, but too late, for when the words left my numbing lips, I heard my baby sister's crash and startled scream as she hit the water.

We ran along beside her as the river took her away. We tried to coax her into grabbing logs or stones or pieces of the bank, but it was no use, for her heavy winter clothes drug her under time and time again, and within a minute, her screaming mouth had taken in too much water and the sounds of her choking breaths as we ran beside her, helpless to pull her out, were too much like my father's had been. The sight of her large eyes as she struggled to stay afloat were too much like his had been as the air was ripped away from him that day. As I ran, I watched my sister die. I saw the moment when it happened, and I swear I felt the icy cold of her hatred for me as her soul rushed past on her way from the living world to wherever it is we go.

"Why didn't you listen?" I watched my mother say to me as we finally collapsed, and my sister's body bobbed away downriver. I watched it as the bright red bird fluttered down upon a stick nearby. I watched it through the long years between that moment and this. I watched as my younger face crumpled in as my mother's desperate hate for me bloomed alight within her voice. She didn't blame me for my father's death, how could she know I didn't help him when I could? But for Greta's death, she did, and I couldn't blame her. Not really. For I blamed me, too.

I watched my young self-try to hold my mother on that long ago Christmas morn, and I watched as the woman pushed the child away from her and screamed out a cry of so much anger and hate and loss into the child's face. I watched as the woman beat her fists against the snowy ground over and over and over again as scream after pain-filled scream continued to fill the air. I watched as the snow began to pinken and then redden beneath those fists as blood began to seep from wounds the pounding made. I watched as the little girl that was me curled up in a ball with her little arms around her knees and tears tracking silently down her grief filled face.

Finally, the bird took flight, and the fog rolled around me. The woman and the child first faded and then were lost to me, and I was once again alone. I felt so sad for that child who had taken on two deaths, who had owned them even though they were not really hers, not entirely, and I hated the child just as much as the mother had. When the third bird came and perched itself upon my shoulder this time, I already knew what I would see. For there was only one other death that I carried with me. There was only one other life that I had helped to take. One other soul that I had damned, so where else could it be that it wanted me to go?

This bird was black from clawed toe to sharpened beak. Its eyes were the glittering of stars within the blackest parts of space, and it didn't need to fly for me to follow. I just went.

I turned and walked, and as I did, I could see the blood begin to take its shape in the fog before my eyes. There was so much bright crimson in the white that it took a while before any other form could make its way into a solid structure within the thickness of the mist. Still, I knew what I would see before I did, so it was no matter, really. For that last sight, there was no smaller me to see. For that last sight had been seen this very day. This very morning.

I had heard my mother leave the house as I had entered. She had begged me not to come, but I could hear the pain within her words, and nothing could have stopped me. Nothing could have kept me from coming.

I rushed on through the house and out the same door she had just gone through, and as I went, I saw the trail of blood she left. The snow was thin in the forest behind her house, but it was enough for the scarlet splashes to shine out like neon in the dark. It was bright enough to make it an easy trail to follow.

Around the trees and down the path I went, and there she had been, sitting on the old bench she had placed before that very same river that had taken my sister from us all those years ago, though miles from the place. This had been the spot they had finally dragged her small form from, and this was where my mom had brought the bench and the place, she had chosen to have her life slowly drain away.

I saw her body sitting there before me on the bench she had painted that same red color as the sled had been. The same bright red color as the blood that dripped from her sliced-open slender wrists. I could hear the dripping as it plip-plopped into the puddle it had formed beneath her, and as I watched, she slowly turned her head.

"You…" she said. Her voice a creak as his had been, and I stepped back away from her, just a step. The look of hate she had for me in her fierce brown eyes was like a dagger to my heart, and as I watched, unable to move, I saw the grimace on her lips loosen and slack, and I watched as the brilliant shine of the life her body held slipped away. Her eyes were one second filled with the spark of anger and loss, and then they were just blank and empty things. Soulless things. And her body slid, just a bit, to one side.

"Mom," I said again, as I had said then, not so long ago, and as the words left my mouth, the raven took flight, and I turned and began to run.

Back through the forest down the path just as I had this morning, and when I got to the house, I ran around it instead of through. Up the drive and to my car, I went, and there was no thought as I put the thing in drive and rushed away. Trying to outrun the added weight of one more death I knew belonged to me. Trying to race away the feeling of knowing that my very being had caused so much grief. So much loss.

I didn't care about the traffic that began to pop up on the road around me. I didn't care about the folks walking down the sidewalks with their stacks of Christmas joy in brightly wrapped boxes in their arms. I just wanted to outrun the pain that chased on after. I just wanted to escape the heaviness of guilt and loss.

The tears flowed from my eyes, blurring my vision and making it impossible to see what was there before me, but it made no difference either way. The only thing that mattered was going faster and faster. Of outracing the bright crimson cloud that followed. Of escaping the heavy knowledge of all the bad there was because of me.

That's when it happened. The sudden stopping and crashing as my car hit another as it crossed the road, its light green when mine was red. That's when my seat beltless body was thrown forward through my windshield, and I flew out into the air, still trying to outrace the guilt that followed.

My body slammed hard into the car that I had hit. My skull smashed into the window on the driver's side door of the shiny red car that was now a crumpled mess. I died so quick I couldn't even hear the sound of those in pain within that metal box, the whimpering they made as their wounds filled their bodies with alarm bells, and blood raced from the injuries my car had caused.

I felt nothing as I stood, my body lying at my feet, but finally, I was able to see what was making all the noises the first bird had taken me from. The father behind the wheel was dying. He looked at me, and I could tell his eyes could see my form staring back at him. His mouth opened and closed just like a fish's when it sits upon the banks, unable to breathe the air of this strange new world it only ever saw in flashes. Bright red blood gushed from his nose where the airbag had broken it, and his face rested against the steering wheel, his hands useless things laying helpless at his sides. The mother screamed and screamed as she saw him lying there, and the children cried and cried from their places in the back.

That's when the fourth bird came. It landed heavy on the hood, and I could hear its talons scraping against the paint as I turned to see what kind this one would be. What kind was sent to collect my soul and weigh its worth. Whatever kind it was, I knew it would find me lacking.

A great horned owl sat there before me; larger than any bird I had ever seen. It hooted softly to itself as our eyes met, and I was relieved at the kindness I saw within. Bright gold rings filled with brownish specks that circled deep black pupils took me in, and I could feel the heaviness of all the guilt I carried being lifted up and off me. I could feel this beast who seemed so wise and fair and kind take on that guilt, and as it did, I knew that wherever I went next, I would deserve and all would be okay, even if there was some hell that this creature sent me to.

I stood there staring at the beautiful feathered beast, and as I did, the mist came back to obscure all there was, but he and I, and I waited. For eons, it seemed we stood there, staring into each other as we did, and finally, the bird took flight. Its wings spread out, taking it away in just a blink, and as it did, I was left alone, and the fog began to thicken.

I thought that maybe now fear would come as the whiteness grew, and I lost myself within. My body was fully gone, and all there was was nothing. But no fear came, and I realized there was also no longer any guilt or pain or sadness. All that was left was peace, and if I could, I would have smiled. For finally, I was free. I was free.

FIVE GOLD RINGS
Kelvin VA Allison

December 24th, 1684
The Five Gold Rings tavern.
Walfinch, High Weald.

"And you are sure that the money is there? In this tomb?" Black Shrew leaned over the table, his voice a harsh whisper, expectation upon his bearded face.

Licking at his dry lips, aware of several heads in the remote moorland inn turning slightly in the direction of their corner table, Milton lifted his face, and turned his countenance upon the curious patrons, watching with satisfaction as each turned away.

Yet what was to be expected of them; they were farmers and labourers; they wanted no trouble from the likes of he and his companions.

Smiling coldly, Milton let his gaze drift among the six men gathered around the table in the gloomy corner of the inn with him, four sitting, two standing. Behind the table, barely visible in the shadows where the two walls met, Richmond of Norfolk was leaning cat-like, arms folded across his chest, a trident beard upon his chin, and his matted hair tied back behind his head, a testament to his time as a privateer.

Beside him, stood Greenaway, the former seaman's brother-in-law, a man as broad and bald as Richmond was lean and hirsute. Greenaway, formerly of Norfolk, was the crude hammer to Richmond's elegant nail, the pair having made their name robbing the roads between Suffolk and Norfolk over the past half decade.

Seated in front of the pair were the brothers, Albert and James Game of Wiltshire, the former staring at Milton with interest while the latter busied himself with stuffing his pipe with tobacco. Studying the pair, Milton found himself wondering if their mother had taken a lover after the birth of the elder Albert. The man stood just five feet seven inches in height but was impossibly broad, his bald head and thick beard making him look more like a brother to Greenaway, while James was stick thin, and tall like willow. Albert was a former priest turned highwayman, a now emotionless force of nature, that seemed to spend most of his time keeping his younger brother from one insane scheme or another.

To the left of James sat Foolish Rake, his trademark lopsided smile upon his features, his fingers clasped together upon the scarred and worn tabletop before them. As Milton studied the man, Foolish Rake gave a stretch and a yawn, his long black hair hanging about his slack-jawed features, his expression adding to the simple appearance that had earned him his nickname. In truth, Foolish Rake was a cold-blooded killer, and the right-hand man of Black Shrew who sat opposite Milton, awaiting an answer to his question.

Forcing himself to focus, Milton turned his gaze back on the man, taking in the cultivated appearance of the man known as the Gentleman of the Road, his long black hair tied back with a ribbon, his black beard meticulously cut, and his clothes, coat, and boots of expensive style.

Milton smiled as he considered what he had learned of the man; of how he was the fifth son of a Cheshire farmer not the outcast son of a lord, of how he cut his own beard, and how he had taken his fine clothes from a drunken aristocrat whose throat he had then cut.

Yet the fact that his entire appearance was a carefully fabricated persona made him no less dangerous. If anything, it was the opposite, several men who had thought that they could bluff or intimidate the 'gentleman highwayman' finding their error too late.

Just as many men had misjudged Milton for similar reasons, assuming that the short man with the big words and the network of informants was no threat, none of them realising that knowledge was power.

Indeed, seated at the table surrounded by scar-faced killers, the five-foot three-inch former military officer was by far and away the most dangerous of them all.

"Well?" Black Shrew pressed, his tone bordering on anger. "Must we wait until Christmas Day to be told?"

"The money is in the tomb, the money, jewels, gold rings, as I promised in my correspondence with each of you," Milton spoke calmly, smoothly. "Everything that I promised is there, sealed tight within the family tomb of the Dalby estate."

"Gold rings," James Game gave a chuckle, glancing up from his pipe. "Like the tavern, eh, like this place?"

"I thought it fitting," Milton smiled at the man.

"What is the cut?" Richmond asked, an eyebrow rising, and Milton gave a shrug as he turned to face him.

"As much as each of us can carry out from the crypt, no more no less. I have brought each of us a sack."

"Sacks?" Richmond blinked. "You make it sound as though we shall be ankle deep in gold and jewels."

"I know, Milton smiled, and Richmond turned to exchange glances with Greenaway in surprise.

"Guarded?" the elder Game brother raised an eyebrow, and Milton shook his head, grinning.

"No, few know of the tomb's existence outside of the family, and they are currently in the north of the country at their second home. There are just servants at the home and the tomb is far from the building."

A heavy silence settled on the table, each of the men exchanging glances, and then Richmond spoke from where he stood in the half-shadows. "But you *do* know of it?"

"Obviously."

"How?" the lean man took a step forward. "Well?"

Milton licked at his lips once more, his gaze drifting to the far side of the tavern where a youth waited nervously, his face dirty and his ginger hair bright. Then Milton gave a shrug. "You expect me to reveal my sources? How unprofessional."

"What did you say little man," Greenaway growled, his brow furrowing as he took a step forward only for a hand of Richmond on his shoulder to stop him at once, the leader of the pair meeting the gaze of Milton.

"I am merely curious; we came a long way on the back of your name. It could have been a trap, we might still end up dancing a jig on a rope, I'd like to know how sure you are that this information you have is reliable."

"Aye," Albert Game nodded, his expression grimmer than before. "And us."

"And you?" Milton didn't bother to keep the sneer from his voice as he let his gaze meet that of Black Shrew.

The Gentleman of the Road gave a humourless smile, shrugging as he sat back. "Why not, as we are in a sharing mood."

Milton raised a hand, not breaking the gaze of the man opposite him, and beckoned the youth to join them.

On shaky legs he came, eyes wide as he stopped beside Milton, and the short man glanced up at him, seeing the fear in his wide eyes. Then he looked back at the gang that he had assembled. "This is Benjiman, the son of the head cook at the home of the Dalby family. He has seen the tomb, has heard the family talk of it, and what it contains, and he wishes to become rich from it."

The young man, barely twenty summers long, seemed to shrink under the gaze of the six men about the table, physically flinching as Black Shrew gave a sneer. "And how pray are you two acquainted. I did not have you down for one who seeks the company of young men, it appears I was wrong."

"I know his mother," Milton replied, refusing to rise to the others attempt to anger him, despite the laughter of Foolish Rake. "I trust the boy."

Another heavy silence, and then Richmond spoke once more. "When do you propose we do the job?"

"Tonight," Milton told him, enjoying the look of surprise upon the faces of each of the men about the table. He let them frown and curse and mutter to themselves for a moment, then when he was satisfied, they were done, he continued. "I trust the boy, yet I do not trust any of you beyond good reasoning. Better to do the job tonight than allow any of us to betray the others and do it alone."

"You would accuse us of treachery?" Black Shrew gave a snarl of offense, though it was as fake as his cultured appearance, and Milton nodded in reply.

"I would, and I would not expect any of you to trust me beyond good reason. If we were to plan this job for five days' time, what is to stop any of us betraying the rest?"

Their silence was all the answer he had sought, and he nodded once more, then turned to Albert as the former priest spoke. "If the tomb is unguarded as you say, then why do you need us? Why not throw some coin at some local muscle and have them do the job for you?"

"There is always safety in numbers, and if the worst were to happen, I would rather find myself aided by cold-blooded killers such as you than thugs."

As several of the men nodded in understanding, Foolish Rake spoke for the first time. "We are highwaymen not grave robbers."

"So, who better?" Milton risked a smile. "Who would think to lay the blame at our door? The Dalby family have influence. They are not people that I would wish coming after me."

"Scared?" Black Shrew sneered, teeth showing.

"Of course," Milton was unashamed. "Fear and caution are what have led me to still be alive."

Another heavy silence settled over their corner of the tavern, then Milton gave a nod. "Gather your gear, my friends for the evening, we have work at hand."

It had already been dark when the groups of men had arrived at the Five Gold Rings Inn, earlier that evening, yet as they rode away from it, it seemed even darker.

They rode in silence, travel cloaks pulled up against the rain that fell on them in sheets, ice cold and biting, and it ran from the three gaps in their tricornes in small rivers.

On they travelled, through the night, following the young man by the name of Benjiman as he rode at their head. Milton rode slightly behind him, knowing that he was offering his back as a target to the six brutal men that followed but knowing that he had little choice if he were to keep them trusting him. A more cautious man might have ridden at the back where he could watch for any sign of danger, but such a man would be viewed with suspicion by those that he hoped to work with. And so, he rode on in silence, confident that none of the men behind him would try their luck. Had it just been Black Shrew and Foolish Rake, he knew that he would be a dead man, but the presence of the pair from Norfolk and the Game brothers was staying their murderous hands.

Indeed, one of the pleasures in organising groups like this was that none of the men knew each other besides reputation and would not try their luck.

Not yet.

That would come later.

He was sure of it.

They passed through several villages, some barely more than a couple of houses with a nearby farm, not stopping at any of them, and they spoke only when clear of such places, and then only in their familiar pairs.

An hour passed by, stretching into the next and then the young man at their head raised a hand, signalling that the others should do the same. The men moved forward, lining their mounts up in a crude line, all eager to hear what their guide had to say. He eyed them in silence for a moment, pale features etched with raindrops, his hair that hung from his hood plastered to his face. Then he pointed with a hand. "Down there, past the trees."

"The Dalby estate," Richmond raised an eyebrow,

and the young man nodded, a tight smile on his thin lips.

"And the tomb?" Black Shrew sneered, drawing the gaze of everyone to where he sat atop his horse.

"A mile inside the grounds," Milton took up speaking. "Hidden within a small copse of oak."

The men nodded, several of them staring off into the dark night ahead of them as if seeing the tomb, and without another word, Milton clicked his tongue, moving his horse onwards, and the others followed.

The rain stopped as they were tethering their horses in a hollow, shielded by a stand of ancient elms, bent, and twisted towards the east, and then like wraiths they slipped across the land in the Christmas Eve moonlight.

For what seemed an age they crossed the open land of the Dalby estate then ahead of them, looming large on the horizon came a darker patch of night.

"There," Benjiman pointed, his face pale as he glanced back at the rough men about him. "The oaks."

On they ran, following the curve of the land as it sloped upwards towards the trees, and Milton found himself nodding in understanding as he studied them.

It had seemed odd to him at first that the Dalby family should build their family crypt amid a copse of trees, where the thick roots would grow and push their way through stone, yet now it all made sense to him.

Yet now he could see that the copse was on a hill, which meant that the crypt had been buried deep in the ground below it, safe from the threat of the encroaching roots, all but hidden from prying eyes.

In truth were it not for the loose tongue of Benjiman, Milton himself would not know of the crypt.

Nor the treasure that lay within.

As he ran silently among the other men, Milton let his mind picture the secret that the Dalby family had been hiding on their grounds, the wealth that their patriarch Sir Bertrand D'Alby had returned from the last crusades with hundreds of years before.

The Kiss of Saladin.

His smile grew as he considered what form it would take; perhaps a crown or tiara, wrought from gold and encrusted with jewels as big as a man's eye, or mayhap it was a sword, as big as a man, with a golden hilt and a blade of diamond. He shuddered as he realised that he would know soon enough, his excitement only tempered by the knowledge that before he could remove it from the tomb there would be bloodshed.

In moments they were amid the trees, each of the men snatching pistols from their cloaks and belts as sudden movement erupted all about them, each certain that they had been captured by the keepers of the estate or by parish summoned constables, only to stare in shock as the herd of red deer that had been sheltering beneath the oaks from the rain, fled into the dark night.

Laughter rippled among them, the good humour of men who had been embarrassed in front of others who had been equally so, and for a brief moment, the strangers were one, united in their humility.

"There!" Black Shrew suddenly thrust an arm to the east dispelling the good humour, and as one the men turned towards a darker patch set back among the oaks.

Together they moved towards it, forming a loose line before what turned out to be little more than a metal gate, sealing off an entrance into the stone block about it, and Greenaway cursing under his breath.

"Damn it all, we need some light!"

"No lights!" Milton snapped, though none had moved to light any. "There will be lanterns in the crypt I would imagine, we can light them once we are within, and not risk being seen by unwelcome eyes!"

The broad man sent him a look that he could not discern in the darkness, and then Milton turned to their guide. "Benjiman, if you would be so kind."

The young man stepped to the fore, squeezing between the killers, and robbers, a hand rising from within his travelling cloak, a large metal key clasped tight between his shaking fingers. Stepping aside, Milton watched as he raised it to the heavy lock, and pushed it inside, a turn of his wrist opening it with a loud click.

The young man withdrew the key, and thrust it back inside his cloak, then pushed at the gate which swung inward on well-oiled hinges, something that drew a look of surprise from the organiser of the night's robbery. Benjiman seemed to sense his thoughts, for he turned towards where the shorter man stood, his voice shaking as he spoke. "The Dalby family often pay their respects to their ancestors; the tomb is well visited."

"Then let us not tarry," Milton advised, stepping past him, a finger pointing. "You will wait here, for our return. Close the gate behind us, lest someone come."

The others shifted uncomfortably at his words, and as he had expected, it was Black Shrew who spoke his mind first. "You would let this boy lock us inside the tomb? What is to stop him from then fetching keepers or constables? Why should we trust him?"

Milton turned, his shoulders shrugging beneath his cloak. "Perhaps you should wait here in his stead."

"And miss my share of the wealth?" Black Shrew gave a smile. "No, I think not. But Foolish Rake shall."

"Oh?" Milton did well to hide the smile that threatened to creep onto his features as his plan began to slot into place like a child's puzzle. Yet he could not let it seem like he was agreeable. "I am not sure…"

"It is not open for discussion," Black Shrew took a step towards him. "My man stays at the gate with the boy. We go down into the crypt…you will lead the way."

As the Norfolk pair and the Game brothers all exchanged glances, and the thin figure of Foolish Rake took a step back, Milton nodded. "As you wish."

Black Shrews chuckle was like leaves blowing in the breeze, his face locked to Milton's as he addressed his assistant. "Stay here, close the gate but do not lock it. If the boy tries anything kill him."

The soft laughter of the cold-blooded killer was all the reply that came and then Black Shrew gestured with a hand. "Lead on Milton. We shall follow."

He nodded, stepping through into the small stone building beyond the metal gate, then turned back as Benjiman spoke, telling him where he could find flint, steel, and tinder. Nodding, Milton felt along the wall to a small alcove, finding the items, then stood for a moment, his body working on muscle memory as he lit the wall sconce that hung upon the wall in a metal bracket.

Lifting the sconce from the wall, careful to hold it by the wooden handle at his base, Milton turned, holding it up.

The stone building ended just feet beyond where Milton stood, yet wide stone stairs led down into the hill upon which the crypt was built, waiting for him like an open mouth, ready to consume him body and soul.

Pushing the thoughts away, he stepped quickly to the top of the stairs and began to descend, aware of the five men moving behind him, the dull clang of the gate closing gently following them down into the crypt.

Milton paused after ten steps as he came across another wall sconce which he lit with the one that he held.

The stairwell grew lighter, and as they continued down the wide stone steps, Milton lit each sconce that they came to until finally, they reached the bottom.

They spread out slowly until the six men were stood in a rough line, their eyes staring at their surroundings, soft gasps and curses escaping their shocked features.

Even Milton who had been made aware of what awaited them by Benjiman found it difficult to focus, his breath catching in his throat as he studied the large crypt.

Treasure sat everywhere, resting upon shelves carved into the stone of the hill, piles of gold coins and jewels stacked carelessly against the walls, filling the corners of the crypt with small mountains of wealth.

"I've died," the voice of the younger Game brother was thick with disbelief. "I've died and gone to heaven…do you see this, Albert, do you see this?"

"Aye," his sibling confirmed with a grunt, his bearded features set with a look of awe. "I see it."

The minutes seemed to drag out before them in silence as they glanced about, heads shaking, and licking at his dry lips, Milton turned to cast a glance at Black Shrew and saw the avarice in the man's eyes, as yet unaware of the problem that he caused for himself.

With a gleeful chuckle, Black Shrew started forwards, hands sinking into a pile of gold coins which he then let pour through his open fingers like water.

With a loud laugh, James Game gave a shout of excitement only to curse and stumble forward as his older brother clouted him across the back of his head with a large hand. "Silence you silly bastard, or you will have trouble down on our heads!"

The younger Game brother scowled at Albert, head starting to shake. "We are too far from the house…"

"But still best to be cautious, my friend," the soft voice of Richmond advised and casting his older brother a grudging look, James threw the former sailor a nod.

"Aye, I suppose so."

The remaining four men moved forward to join the Black Shrew, sifting through the treasure, yet Milton stayed where he was, watching as they began to fill the sacks that he had provided them with on leaving the Inn.

Then he began to walk around the crypt, holding the sconce in his hand high as he read the inscriptions carved into the stone above each tomb set into the walls.

On he moved, aware of the others casting him curious glances, wondering why he was not filling his own sack, yet he ignored them all, intent on finding that which he had arranged this night to gain possession of.

His breath caught in his throat as he saw it, five gold rings in a line carved into the stone above a gated doorway, each ring linked to the one preceding it.

The Kiss of Saladin.

Unable to control himself, he rushed towards it, a shaky hand rising to snatch the metal key from the hook beside the door, apparently left there so that the Dalby servants were able to clean the inside of the crypt.

For this was the personal tomb of Sir Bertrand D'Alby.

The lock clicked open easily, and filled with almost childlike glee, Milton pushed the gate open to reveal what a short stone tunnel, a stone sarcophagus at its end, bathed in thick shadow, the flickering flames of his sconce casting patterns on the walls.

Staring at the tomb of the knight, Milton was filled with gleeful mania, for with this wealth he could claim the place in society that had long been denied him.

For he was the secret bastard child of the former Lord Protector of England, Oliver Cromwell, raised in secrecy and shame, told of his heritage upon his father's death.

He had tried to reach out to his siblings then, only to be turned away by his eldest brother Richard, the new Lord Protector of England on pain of death.

Yet now, now all of that would change.

"Hold!" the deep voice of Greenaway snarled behind Milton, thick with anger. "We were promised just one sack to a man!"

So it had begun as he had known it would.

Holding his breath, Milton continued to stare into the tomb before him, only turning as he heard the click of a gun, and the sneer of Black Shrew. "You dare?"

Black Shrew stood on one side of the crypt, one hand clutching tight to the neck of a bulging sack, while his other pointed a pistol at a red-faced

Greenaway, the large man pointing his own weapon back in return.

As Milton stood watching, James Game moved as if to speak only to fall silent as his brother raised a hand, and then Richmond of Norfolk pointed his own pistol at Black Shrew, his tone pleasant. "Drop the gun!"

"Treachery!" Black Shrew snarled; his features twisted in hatred. "Traitors to a man!"

Milton studied the group for a moment, then took a step forward. "Is there a problem?"

"He was filling two sacks!" Greenaway spat, eyes narrowing as he glared at Black Shrew. "You said that we could take one sack each, all that a man could carry!"

"I did indeed," Milton smiled. "The only rule."

"What?" Black Shrew shook his head. "Foolish Rake guards the gate above!"

"I believe you chose for him to stay there," Milton stated, shrugging as he spoke. "Your choice."

Realisation suddenly grew in Black Shrews eyes, and he cursed, the gun swinging towards Milton. "You planned this...you wanted this to happen!"

Milton blinked innocently. "Come now..."

Licking at his dry lips, Black Shrew turned his head, seeing that the guns of Richmond and Greenaway were still upon him, then turned his gaze to the Game brothers. "You two…join me…we can kill these three and take all this for ourselves! We can all be rich!"

"A man can only use so much money," Albert Game drew his own weapon, and pointed it at Black Shrew, distaste on his features. "I think not!"

"Speak for yourself brother!" the younger Game brother drew his gun and pointed it at his older sibling as he took a step back, addressing Black Shrew as he spoke. "I am with you!"

"Stupid boy!" Albert snarled, head turning to glare at his brother though his gun stayed where it was.

"Don't call me that!" James roared back.

Milton stood and watched it all, silent as the grave, a smile playing along his thin lips, having known that it would end in bloodshed from the start.

He felt more than heard the presence of the thing behind him, the creature that had crept silently from within the tomb of the knight, Sir Bertrand D'Alby.

Milton spun on his heels, eyes wide as he stared at the figure before him, the leathery skin of its face staring back at him from amid the stained bandages wrapped about its head, its powerful form clad in an equally stained long tabard bearing the insignia of the

Dalby family, and a crusader cross, all illuminated by the sconce he still held. "What in…"

Time stretched away as he stared into its bright blue eyes, seeing the intelligence within them, then he screamed as it grasped him with strong hands, lifting his form from the floor as it snapped its teeth at his face.

He turned his head at the last moment, his scream intensifying as teeth tore deep through his right cheek.

Without warning, he was thrown aside, dropping the sconce as he flew. He struck the wall beside the steps leading up and fell heavily, grunting in pain as he felt several ribs break within him. Gasping in agony, blood running down his face, Milton raised his gaze to stare at the scene before him, head shaking in denial.

As one, Greenaway and Richmond both turned, firing their weapons at the living corpse, their attacks putting dark holes in its chest but nothing more, then the bigger of the men staggered back as Black Shrew turned and shot him. As Greenaway fell, Richmond turned to scream at Black Shrew. "Treacherous bastard!"

Then the creature was upon him, hands grasping the man by the shoulders as it bent its head and tore his throat free in a torrent of blood that splattered noisily down on the flagstones at their feet.

Another gunshot roared, and Milton turned his head, watching in genuine shock as Albert took two unsteady steps back against a wall, and dropped to one knee as his free hand clasped at his left side. Smoke billowing from his gun, James took a step toward his brother. "Albert…I never meant to…"

His words were cut off as Albert raised his gun, the crack of his pistol loud, the head of James jerking back as the shot took him through his right eye. He fell, his legs folding beneath him, and his head making a sickening crack as it struck the stone floor hard.

Hissing through his teeth, Albert forced himself to his feet and turned, meeting the gaze of Milton as he lay beside the steps. He nodded, teeth set, and turned to rush at the creature that was still feeding on Richmond, the former priest muttering a prayer as he charged. With a mind-numbing snarl, the creature cast the limp body of Richmond aside, its mouth and chest thick with blood and gore, and stepped to meet the threat.

Movement snatched at Milton's attention, and he turned, watching in disbelief as Black Shrew charged across the crypt, his own sack in one hand, then paused to grab those of James and Albert from the ground. As he straightened, they made eye contact, and the dark-haired man gave a cruel smile then raced for the stairs as best as he could under the weight of his bounty.

Grimacing against the pain in his body, Milton turned back to the struggle before him, watching in horror as the creature shrugged off a powerful punch from Albert Game, then gripped the man's fist and tore his right arm from his body. The highwayman grunted in shock as the limb was cast aside, his blood arcing up the nearest wall, and then the creature was upon him, bundling him down to the stone floor, teeth snapping.

Forcing himself to rise, Milton took a step up the stairs away from the fight, blood running over his bottom lip as he coughed, fire lancing through his lungs.

In the chamber, the creature had its face buried in the belly of Albert, grey fingers shovelling bloody gobbets of meat and internal organs into its mouth as it moaned in pleasure, like an aristocrat at a banquet.

Milton took another step back.

Then it turned and grinned at him.

Milton choked back a sob of terror, agony coursing through him as he began to clamber up the stone steps. In his haste he fell, yet still he continued on his hands and knees, fingers clawing at the steps before him, several fingernails tearing themselves loose.

The top of the stairs came into sight as he turned a corner, and before the gate, Black Shrew spun from where he was stood, his sacks of plunder about him.

Snarling, Black Shrew fired his weapon, and Milton gasped as the shot buzzed past his face, close enough to feel the hot air, and on instinct he dragged free the gun that he had forgotten was hidden within his coat until that moment and returned fire.

Black Shrew shrieked in pain, hands clasping to his stomach as he dropped his gun, and fell, rolling head over heels as he crashed down the stairs past Milton.

Below in the crypt something scuffed on stone, and filled with a renewed energy, he forced himself back to his feet, hands clinging to the stone wall as he climbed the stone steps towards the metal gate ahead,

"Benjiman!" he called out, no longer caring if he were to be heard from the house, his fear of the creature below supplanting all else. "Open the gate, boy!"

The gate shook as he struck it, hands grasping to the curves of its design, then cursed loudly as he caught sight of Foolish Rake lying upon the ground in a dark pool of blood, the killers throat slashed open.

Movement behind him in the stairwell made Milton turn, a squeal of childlike terror escaping him as he saw Black Shrew crawl back into view from where he had fallen, empty sockets where his eyes had once been, blood pouring from his now tongueless mouth.

Milton stepped back into the gate with a clang as the creature moved into view behind Black Shrew, and perhaps sensing its presence, the blind man sobbed loudly, a tortured moan of terror escaping him.

Without a word, the creature fell upon him, hands ripping the clothes from the man as his teeth found the flesh beneath as it fed hungrily, feeding upon the meat of his belly and the organs within. Then its fingers found his eyes and mouth, grasping his head tight as they cracked his skull to get the hidden delicacy.

Milton watched it all with a detached sense of terror, a sob escaping him every now and then as a new depravity from inflicted upon the corpse of the man that he had wanted dead above all others, a business rival.

A soft footstep behind him made him spin about, hope taking flight within his broken body as he saw Benjiman move into sight, a knife clasped in a hand.

"Boy?" Milton blinked, then his gaze dropped to the body of Foolish Rake, understanding flooding him.

The boy had killed Black Shrew's accomplice.

But why? Had the man tried to murder him?

Benjiman stayed silent, his eyes drifting past Milton to stare down the stone steps, and the older man was jerked back to the threat at hand, his fingers shaking the metal gate. "Open it now, let me out!"

"Don't you want it?" the reply came, and Milton blinked, confused not just by the question but by the change in personality of the previously nervous youth.

Not that he knew him well, at all.

He had not known the boys' mothers as he had claimed, and only knew of the crypt and the treasure contained within after Benjiman had come to him.

The rest had been but a ruse to convince the others of his faith in the boy, so desperate had he been to get his hands upon the riches within the crypt.

"The kiss of Saladin," Benjiman smiled, head tilting to one side within his hood. "Don't you want it?"

Milton blinked, head turning to stare at the creature as it began to slowly climb towards him, his eyes once more settling upon the insignia upon the blood-soaked tabard that it wore. "Sir Betrand D'Alby."

He could hear the smile in the voice of Benjiman as he spoke. "Indeed, returned home from the crusades with his ailment, the Kiss of Saladin, after being bitten by a similar creature in the tunnels beneath the Holy City of Jerusalem."

"Damn your eyes," Milton turned to stare at the young man, his gaze dropping as he saw the three sacks of treasure that Black Shrew had left before the closed gate. "Open it now, and I swear you can own it all."

"Oh, but I already do," Benjiman chuckled softly.

"I…I don't understand…"

Benjiman nodded and stepped away from the gate, a smile creasing his features. "I am the last living heir to the Dalby estate, and I do what must be done to protect my family name and do right by my ancestors."

"Do right?" Milton's voice was hysterical as he felt the creature move to stand behind him, his hands rattling the gate but then it was upon him, his scream turning to a gargled choking as its teeth found his throat.

Features etched with amusement, Lord Benjiman Dalby stood and watched as his ancestor ate, all but tearing the last of the highwaymen inside out in his never-ending search to quench his hunger, the young man's thoughts on what lay ahead for him.

As always after such a large feast, his ancestor would go catatonic, and would then be placed back inside his tomb, locked away until he awoke once more, and his pained moans of hunger began to grow too loud.

Then Lord Benjiman would venture forth once more with his tales of treasure, and the Kiss of Saladin, searching for greedy men to feed another's hunger.

SIX GEESE A-LAYING
D.W. Hitz

If Elliot Bower understood what the cracking sound beyond the tree line was, he would have stopped there. Being that it was two days before Christmas and his meat freezer was still empty, he wasn't about to stop when there was a sound that could have meant dinner. Though, he was cautious after having his hunting license permanently revoked for poaching.

But that was all bullshit. He may have killed four too many elk last season according to the law, but they had to cheat to prove it, hiding trail cams behind branches and raiding his hunting cabin. Yeah, they knew if they came at him directly, he'd've blown their goddamn heads off and left them for the wolves and the bears, but that didn't justify them coming at him like a bunch of pussies.

Either way, that wasn't going to stop Elliot. He'd been hunting in Custer Falls Nation Forest since he could walk. Top to bottom, from the eastern wash that marked the border of the unincorporated county to the western edge on the summit of Mount Dagbourne. Whether it was in the river, the falls, around the lake, or the thousands of acres of deep wilderness—this was his land, and he had a right to any animal on it.

So that sway of the brush, the snap of a twig ahead—whatever made that noise was his.

As the overcast sky churned ahead, he moved through a stand of Douglas Firs, and the rushing sound of the river swelled in his ears. He grew a little curious about how he had noticed that cracking sound over the ruckus of the rapids. The white noise was coming from beyond the next group of trees, and he pictured it in his mind. The river bent there, changing direction as it crossed a couple hundred boulders from south-southwest to more of a smoother southerly flow. It was a rapid that most of the year, you didn't want to cross, especially in the spring. But the current should have been near its slowest now, the lake readying itself to freeze over and the river winding down to hibernate into a trickle. But it was a warm December this year.

Elliot slowed as he reached the last Doug Fir, leaning against it and clutching his rifle's strap. He watched the clear, crisp waters run over the rocks and scanned the banks on both sides. There were some elk tracks across the river, but it was too dangerous to cross here, and they looked muted within the snow— not fresh. He saw a pile of bear shit a few feet down from where he stood, but it wasn't steaming, just resting in the snow—the sound wasn't from that either.

He stood as still as he could, listening.

The ringing in his ears from his forty-six years of life and his resistance to using any kind of hearing protection when shooting was oppressive over the quietness of nature below the rapid's roar. It was a near-constant bell, slightly less in his right than left, and he just wished it would stop for one goddamn minute so he could hone in on whatever had made that sound.

Nearly two minutes passed before anything happened. That was okay. If there was one thing he'd learned about hunting, it was to have patience. Then, there it was.

A small sound. A rustling. Something brushing against the peaks of dead grass clumps that stood above the snow.

Elliot spun to his right to catch it.

He expected to see the tail of a ground squirrel, a chipmunk, or a rabbit. He wasn't picky today (he was hungry), and Shanice would skin and cook whichever he brought home. But he didn't see any of those. What he saw was the murky brown and black tail of a bird.

He thought he knew exactly what it was the second it flashed its feathers and vanished into the snowy brush, though it didn't make any sense. All the Canadian Geese had passed through and shouldn't have been back until spring, not unless this one was dumb—*Or injured!* His mind flashed with the image of a golden brown, crispy-skinned goose dinner. His mouth salivated at the idea. He hadn't eaten a Canadian Goose in years. It seemed like those damned wardens were always thick in the woods whenever the bird was around.

Well, that was going to change today.

Elliot slid his rifle from his shoulder and rested it against the tree. He couldn't use that. He'd shot a bird with it before, and once all the feathers had settled, there was practically no meat remaining. It had painted the tree behind it in globs of red pureed meat, and almost nothing was left on the bone. He'd do better this time. He slid his .45 from his holster and stepped toward the tall grass the bird had disappeared into.

One slow step at a time, Elliot gritted his teeth. His boots crunched in the stiff snow. The bird may be dumb, but if he made too much noise, he was sure he'd lose it.

He held the tops of the grass to one side and saw a trail into a four-foot-tall mess of brambles. He followed, ducking as he neared, seeing a hole in the dried vegetation. It was a little taller than his knees—it had to be where the thing was nesting.

Crouching on his knees, he leaned down. One gloved hand on the ground to support himself, the other pointing his pistol into the hole, he squinted.

He saw the brown and tan and black that could have been the bird, but nothing making a definitive shape, nothing showing him where to aim. Sure, he could just fire, but what if the shot just went through its feathers? What if he was mistaking darkened shadows for the bird? It could flap its wings and fly away. He'd be left with nothing. No, he needed a clean shot.

He leaned closer, pressed the edge of his pistol against the brush, and held the gap open a hair larger. In the heavens, the clouds parted ever so slightly, letting a band of sun through the thick layers of gray.

He thought it would be helpful at first. He saw a little deeper into the brush. But in a flash, the entire brightness of the day fell on his face, and the darkened space in front of him was black, the snow, a bright white that blinded him.

Elliot pulled back, covering his eyes, and the weirdest sound raged in his ears.

It reminded him of horns on those old cars from black and white movies, but instead of a car, he was hit with a sledgehammer made of feathers and a chomping black beak.

It bit into his hand, and the pistol dropped into the snow. The bite was hot, shooting up his arm, and while he thought he knew what was happening, it made no sense. Sure, geese can be aggressive—he'd even been bitten on the shin before—but the bite of this one...

Not a second passed, and it was biting his arm. The beak ripped into his coat, through shell and lining, and the force of its snap felt like he was wearing nothing at all.

He scooted back. It was ridiculous. He was being attacked by a goose, and it was making him flee. But he was honestly scared. What could he do? His hand was on fire as if he'd been injected with venom. His arm was screaming, and the thing was advancing on his face, pecking the air and honking as it moved.

"Fuck!" Elliot rolled to his left, away from the thing, tried to stand, and it bit into his leg.

It felt like a punch, like someone had snuck up behind him and thumped him in the hamstring. He dropped back to the ground, his leg both numb and filling with fire.

"You fucking bird!" He rolled harder, faster. He had to get away from this thing. It was just a stupid fucking bird. How it had wrecked his arm and his leg, he couldn't explain, but he had to get away.

Another thump, the same leg, and it was all but dead now. Fire surged over his hips. And another in his other leg.

He screamed and fell back against the snow, flapping wings rushing toward his face. He felt the river splashing to his side, drops of thirty-three-degree water raining onto his face and freezing his skin.

"Fuck!"

He moved his left hand using nothing but pure instinct. He had little sight of the bird and no plan whatsoever.

He thrust it over his chest as flapping wings swatted his face. The black bill of the beast dove toward his right eye, and Elliot seized the thing's neck in his grip.

Wings smacked his face. Its feet dug into his belly, ripping his coat. Feathers and synthetic stuffing fluttered into the air like snow in some far-off dream where flakes fell like the down of a busted pillow.

"Die!" He squeezed. He expected to hear a crack, to feel it between his fingers as the bird's neck gave to his superior human will. But it didn't. It snapped its beak, getting closer and closer to his skin, and he knew from the other bites that if it connected, he'd likely lose his hold (and his eye).

He moved again without thinking.

Elliot spun and plunged the bird into the river, the back of its neck, then its entire head.

His hand froze almost instantly. His fingers were numb and aching. He felt nothing where his digits were wrapped around the thing, but still, he squeezed as hard as he could as water splashed from wings, feet flailed, and bleats of goose rage crashed through bubbles up to the surface. Until they didn't. Until bubbles ceased, and a few seconds later, so did its wings and legs.

But still he held it under. His heart throbbed, and some part of him knew if he brought it up too fast, it would cough and honk and come right after him again.

So, he waited, and his fingers burned. His entire hand burned from the cold. It crept up his forearm and chilled his entire body.

Elliot's rage wanted to pull the thing out and toss it away, to be rid of the trouble the damned thing had caused him. But spite raised its head and said, *No, you need to eat him. Pay that fucker back for biting you.*

"Fuck, yeah."

He pulled the bird from the water and stared into its eyes. It didn't cough or fight. It watched him with a dead, graying gaze.

"Fuck you." He tossed it onto the snow.

It took a good half hour before his hand was warm. By then, the feeling had returned to his legs and arm, and he brushed off the blows as the damn bird somehow hitting nerve endings or pressure points or some shit. It had just gotten lucky.

He walked to the carcass, lying beside the entrance to its nest, and he leaned down to seize his prize, his gaze falling into the brush. There was an urge as he did this, something that made him wonder, just what was inside that patch of brambles where it had come from?

Elliot crawled to the opening, picked up his pistol, and slid it into his holster. He lowered his face and peered deep inside the enclave of dried, thorny branches and tangles of tall grasses. What he saw was a clutch of six eggs.

"Well, shit."

A disgusted feeling slipped over Elliot. In a normal person, this may have been guilt, but he didn't feel that. It was more of a feeling that he almost fucked up and left them behind.

Elliot wriggled closer and gathered each egg. It was weird—he wouldn't deny that—a bird with a nest full of eggs in winter. It was out of season for geese to do that unless they were farm-bred. He firmed that idea in his head; it must have had a daddy or granddaddy that was farm-raised, or it had somehow escaped, that's all. His gain.

Each egg found a spot in his coat pockets, the rifle went back on his shoulder, and the bird hung by the neck in his grip, and he slinked back out of the forest.

*

Shanice Trent picked her nose and wiped a long, slimy, pale green winner on the seat of Elliot's chair. She wasn't allowed to sit in it when he was home, but since the couch had barely a hair's width of stuffing left inside it, it was her seat when he was gone. She glanced at the green streak beside her ass, right where his would rest, and she hoped it found a new home on his rump the next time he kicked her off.

Moans came from the television, and her slick fingers found their way back inside her underwear, sliding over her clit. She pinched it hard as she watched Santa (really a brown-haired fat man in a red suit) plow his ten-inch whopper into the ass of a girl in big plastic elf ears. The elf sucked on a candy cane and squealed as he slapped the side of her ass.

Shanice moaned back and slapped the man in the boat, wishing she had a candy cane of her own to slide up in there. The sweet peppermint would go so good with her own salty-sour snatch.

She licked her fingers, and hearing the rumble of Elliot's truck outside, she grabbed the remote and smashed the power button. She may have been horny, but the last thing she was in the mood for right now was Elliot's crusty pecker. Maybe if he brought her something nice, but other than that, she wasn't in the mood (for him).

The door flew open, and Elliot staggered inside, a dead bird dangling from his right hand.

"What the hell is that?" She shuffled in his seat, mindful of the green stripe beside the edge of her panties.

"It's a fucking goose!" He threw the bird across the room, and she had to raise her palms in self-defense to keep it from crashing into her face.

"Fucker!" She smacked it down to the floor, shock and a smile creeping over her face.

"And these." He closed the door and, one by one, placed the eggs on the table.

She watched them wobble on the grimy oak. They were larger than chicken eggs and had green specks peppering their pale-green shells. They reminded her of the present she had left Elliot in the chair, and though she was hungry, the sight made her stomach clamp down. Something seemed to be warning her: Stay away from those fucking eggs.

Elliot dropped his torn coat and boots beside the door. "Well—get the fuck to it."

"What?" She realized she had stiffened, frozen in her stare at the six oblong prizes.

"Get the fuck out of my chair, and go pluck that bird. I want goose tonight."

She shook her head and stood, taking the goose by the feet to the kitchen. She was barely out of the room when Elliot plopped down, smearing the green goober into his ass.

"And these," he shouted, pointing at the eggs. "Get them in the fridge before they spoil. I want goose eggs for breakfast tomorrow."

She left the bird in the sink and came back for the eggs. He smacked her ass hard as she bent to pick them up. She let it slide. He did bring home dinner, after all. Maybe she'd let him slide it in after she was full.

*

Shanice was not an experienced plucker. She'd helped with a chicken or two on her grandmother's farm when she was little—like seven or eight—but never had she done this in her adult life by herself. She did, however, have YouTube and a large pot, and after dipping the goose in super-hot water and yanking clump after clump of feathers from the carcass, she finally had a plucked bird. And a kitchen covered in feathers.

She thought the skin color was a bit odd, somewhat greenish, and asked Elliot. His only response had been *cook the fucking thing*. He said it was hell killing it, and he wanted a damn plate of fried goose in an hour, or else.

Shanice knew he wouldn't hit her—the man was all bark—but she also didn't want to deal with his shit. Last week, she had to sleep on the couch for three days after forgetting to pick up the case of beer he'd asked for—Arney and Joel were coming over for poker, and it was Elliot's turn for the suds. She'd had to go back out since he wasn't going to leave his company to do that. All night it was, "Honey, grab me a beer," or, "Sugar-tits, fetch me the chips," and she complied. It still wasn't enough to keep her spot in the bed.

She gutted the thing and butchered it. Some egg, some flour, salt and pepper, and a skillet full of grease, and she just made her one-hour deadline. They sat in front of the TV, Elliot watching the same fishing show he always tortured her with, and they ate a good half of the bird. She cleaned up their plates and brought him a beer, wrapped the remainder in aluminum foil and set it in the fridge, and she lay down on the couch.

She could feel the meal sitting on her insides like sludge gripping the interior of her gut. The sight of green skin came to mind, but that thought vanished as Elliot burped hard for a solid thirty seconds.

She couldn't help but laugh and stare.

He grinned, rubbing his belly. "You like that?"

She giggled and nodded.

"Then get over here." He shuffled his waist, unzipping his jeans and pushing them down. His crusted-over penis stood up through the opening in his boxers—not that it was hard, the boxers were so old they had shrunk, and any minor movement caused Mr. Winky to slip out.

She watched the dried yellow grime as his member throbbed. He was thinking about her, trying to force himself hard, and his urethra opened and closed as he flexed like a drowning fish.

It wasn't appealing, but she didn't get to finish before he came home earlier, and the thoughts of that ten-inch Santa cock and a candy cane were pretty fresh in her mind. Besides, she'd tasted Elliot's crust when it was three times as thick. Sure, it was bitter and smelled like molded cheese, but he was usually pretty quick to harden, and then it'd be inside her.

She crawled off the sofa, making a show of it. She was some kind of jungle cat, approaching him with hunger on her mind. She waved her ass as she moved closer and kneeled at the base of his chair.

"Oh, yeah." He shifted his pelvis closer to the seat's edge, setting his hands on the armrests and looking down on her like some slave girl sent to service him.

She grabbed her shirt from the bottom seem and lifted it over her head, letting her tits fall free. She licked her fingers and squeezed her nipples, and for a brief moment before she took his cock in hand, she thought her skin was looking a little green.

It was just the light; she knew that. The light and that stupid fishing show.

Her lips and her fingers were still coated in grease as she swallowed his limp dick. It helped clear off the crust and made it a little salty. By the time he was hard, his pre-cum leaked with a green tinge. There was a definite rotten odor that brought the thought of death to mind, but that didn't matter anymore. She didn't have to taste it once it was inside her.

*

Six eggs sat in a red plastic bowl on the refrigerator's top shelf. It was a strange place for them to be, without their mothers, without the open breeze and the crisp smell of fir trees wisping by. It was a situation they conversed about, though not scared at first—their mothers had left to retrieve food in the past—but as time passed and the tall, two-legged thing reached in and set down a platter of meat, a panic set it.

The meat, after all, smelled like mothers. The breath of the two-legged thing smelled like mothers. And as the human shut the door and the light went out, they understood what must be done.

The golden fried meat jostled on its plate until dozens of green dots appeared along its surfaces. Each dot bulged and rippled and grew outward into tiny threads, dozens of green tendrils reaching from the pile of golden fried poultry in different directions.

It wasn't long before the eggs cracked.

*

Elliot wasn't good at fucking. He didn't have an exceptionally large cock, either. It was more of a nub, but it was wide, and he'd learned to put his fingers on the clit and play that son of a bitch like a violin. At least the shuddering and the shaking he got from Shanice made him feel that way. He'd never actually asked.

She'd started on top of him reverse cowgirl in his chair, but he didn't feel like his nub was getting quite as deep as he wanted it to. He pushed her, and they slid to the floor, where he thrust from behind. There was a period of time where he could have sworn, she was saying something about Santa, so he followed up with, "Ho, ho, ho, bitch," right as he came.

If he could have seen what happened inside her, the night might have gone a little differently. As it was, though, when his pale green slime raced past his pus-leaking bumps into the inner walls of her vagina, all he could think was, *Fuck, yeah, I rocked her shit.*

*

While Elliot collapsed onto his chair, feeling like he'd achieved some immortal status in the hallowed halls where the records of fucking were kept, Shanice got to her feet. It may have been winter, but she was hot, and the sludgy feeling in her stomach hadn't moved. What she needed was a beer.

Her tits swaying and green leaking from between her thighs, she headed for the kitchen.

"Grab me a beer while you're in there," Elliot shouted as he lifted the remote and rewound the last five minutes of fishing he'd missed.

"Yeah, yeah." She sighed and grabbed the refrigerator handle, hoping to Christ there was more than one in there.

Shanice imagined the wall of cold about to flood over her naked flesh as she pulled on the door. She braced for it, knowing it would hit the thousands of sweat droplets that clung to her skin and instantly cool her. She was about to close her eyes and let the refreshment have its way with her when a flash of what looked like green webbing caught her attention.

It was like a balloon of snot had exploded and hardened. Green lines stretched from the shelf to the walls to the roof to the eggs. Questions ran through her mind, along with images of an M80 she'd once seen explode a cantaloupe, sending strings of orange across the yard. But she'd heard nothing. And this was green. And the green was similar in color to—

A flash of movement in the back of the fridge. Something closer, and two beer bottles clinked together.

"What the fuck?"

A shiver washed Shanice from head to toe, but it wasn't from the cold. Something was desperately wrong here. She grabbed her breasts to shield them. Something bad was about to—

A drop of green fell from the gap between Shanice's thighs, and before it touched the grimy linoleum floor, several things happened all at once. A flurry of green, a blur with a hundred legs, shot from the bottom of the fridge and climbed onto her foot. She was going to scream—she opened her mouth to, and another blur leaped from the top of the refrigerator door and into her mouth. It was slime-covered, and tendrils whipped at her face as it dove down her throat, each lashing splitting her skin wide, stinging, and burning the open layers of flesh.

She gagged as the wet, slippery thing whipped the insides of her throat, gripped the tunnel ahead with claw-like hooks, and squirmed down. The pain made her forget the thing scaling her legs until its burning limbs reached into her vagina, hooked into her, and dragged itself inside.

She thumped onto her ass. Four green things slithered from the fridge. Slime streaked the floor behind them, as one by one, they hooked into Shanice's holes and reeled themselves inside her.

*

Elliot scratched at his dick. It was mostly dry now, and the crust was reforming. Flakes of yellow and green fell like snow across the stained surface of his chair.

"Shanice! Where's my beer?"

He fondled his balls, the right one feeling bloated and the left smaller and pointed on both ends.

"Shanice!"

She didn't answer.

There was a sound behind him, something like scurrying feet. He thought he'd better put out the mouse traps again before bed; he didn't want to listen to that all night or have another one bite into his face while he was sleeping.

He turned toward the kitchen. "Sha—" His voice went hoarse as he saw what was on the top corner of his chair: a strange green thing that looked something like an emerald jellyfish, its tentacles hanging from the back and sides.

Its tendrils swung toward him, snagging his bottom lip.

He let out a muffled sound as the thing shot from the chair into his mouth. Something slimy crawled across his hand. It was another one. Another climbed up his leg, and he stood. He had to get away from this.

He shook his hand and jumped away from his chair, but the things didn't move. He grabbed the one in his mouth, and it slipped right through his grasp, sliding down his throat.

Elliot gagged. It was filling his lungs, and he could barely breathe, but he wasn't coughing it out— why wasn't he coughing it out?

The one on his foot shot up his leg and snagged his balls in its tentacles. Searing pain, the likes of which he had never imagined, ripped through his guts, and he wanted to puke. He reached for it, and the one on his hand jumped onto his face, squeezing itself into his nostril.

It burned. Everywhere it burned.

He looked down, and the one on his balls was stretching open the crusty urethra while tendrils dove inside him.

He grabbed the slimy thing on his dick and pulled.

Blood ran from his penis, and gashes ripped into his scrotum. The agony, the burning, was blinding, and Elliot lost all control, slamming face-first into the wood floor.

Blood gushed as his nose collapsed from the impact. A geyser ran down his throat, the hole clogged from smashed meat.

But it was better than his balls because while his hands seemed useless to reach down there and fix it, and the slimy green thing ripped his pee-hole wider and cranked itself inward, another one seized the gash in his scrotum and clawed its way in there. And yet another ripped his asshole wide, slipped its limbs inside and anchored them, and pulled itself into him.

Elliot's body convulsed. His head slammed into the floor until his face ripped into pieces. His insides burned from his nuts to his throat, but for a moment, he thought he could relax. However bad, he could breathe again. However painful it was as they ripped into his intestines, tore apart his stomach and liver, and however much he thought he would drown as his lungs filled with blood, his face was calm. Until a final beasts crawled into view.

Elliot wanted to beg. He wanted to say, *Please, no.* But his mouth didn't work.

Tendrils seized his right eye. The thing tried pulling itself inside him, but the organ came loose and shot into the tiny monster's grasp.

Elliot watched in horror as the eye seemed to be enveloped within the creature and dissolve into nothing but blood and gelatinous matter.

Then, it slid across the floor and seized his other eye. He didn't know if the first one had sparked its taste, but he was convinced now that these things wanted to torture him, that was for sure.

It pulled itself into his ocular cavity, surrounding the orb, his face feeling like it would melt from the burning.

The last thing Elliot saw was a green blob as his brain swelled into fire.

*

The front door of Elliot Bower and Shanice Trent's trailer opened on Christmas Eve morning to what could have been argued to be the most beautiful winter day this year. Through the overcast sky, rays of sunlight highlighted the snow-topped peaks of the Custer Range, and the powder-coated trees swayed in the cool easterly breeze.

Six goslings fluttered through the doorway. They wavered in the cold morning air, but only briefly before they found their wings and soared. They flew west toward Custer Falls National Park.

It was several hours before Elliot and Shanice emerged. Their dripping green eyes led them toward town.

Seven Swans a Swimming
Lisa Hutchinson

Gregory

Gregory Hume could not quite believe that he had gotten to this moment. Spending his days as an engineer, for years he had believed he had been destined for greater things. Despite how successful he was in his field; he had a vision. Looking into the mirror, he frowned. Sweat had already begun to seep through the crisp white shirt that he had meticulously ironed to perfection for the occasion. His messy light brown hair had stuck to his forehead. The man could feel the anxiety building. He needed tonight to be perfect, and these small details could ruin everything for him. Eyeing his reflection, he told himself not to be too worried.

An excellent planner such as himself Is came prepared. He had an identical white shirt hanging behind him. He knew that even if he managed to sweat through another, his suit jacket would hide the stains anyway. His hair would just have to do. At the end of the day, he knew he was not the star of the show. As the creator, he was merely there to take in the magic of the evening and embrace the praise that he hoped to gain from the performance.

Checking out the brightly lit room around him, he had to admit he was a little disappointed. Before him, the only mirror to the room stood above a dressing table, which had been left littered with make-up. With a shake of his head, he sighed, he found such mess frustrating. It had always irritated him. As a child, had he left things laid around the house, he would gain a clip around the head from his mum. She was firm. Despised mess. He knew he had inherited that from her. A table and two chairs against one wall and a couch in the centre of the room were the only other items the room had to offer, but being his directional debut, he could not complain.

"On to bigger and better things Gregory old chap!" he said, grinning at himself as he once again admired his reflection before him. Despite the excessive sweating he was currently undergoing, he couldn't complain. At forty-four, he was still blessed with a good head of hair, his father's balding appearing to have skipped him for now.

He used this to his advantage and let it flow freely, waves falling to just below his clean-shaven jaw. Rubbing his hand from his cheek to his smooth chin, he took a moment to consider how his performers were getting on.

Were they as nervous as he was?

He doubted it.

He had chosen each one because they were perfect for the part, and being the perfectionist that he was, he demanded elegance and grace. Each of the women he had chosen had been faultless.

He knew the minute he had seen them, and he just hoped that they were taking their roles as seriously as he was the directing. He had promised each girl that this recital alone would be one that would get them noticed, Swan Lake was an astounding Ballet Performance after all.

Especially to Gregory.

Classical music had always been his go to, musical genre, even as a child. He had been in love with the idea of one person being in full control of an entire room. Every musician waiting for their cue, that conductor perfecting the show. He often wondered if that had fuelled his desire to direct.

The man had grown up surrounded by swans. Swan ornaments lined his home as a child. His mother had always adored them. She herself was slender and graceful. Choosing to dress herself head to toe in white. Much to the boy's amusement, he found in her frustration that she at times sounded like the hissing bird. This show was to be his ultimate dedication to her. To the woman that had given him life, raised him with morals and respect. She had always been a difficult woman to please, and he hoped this would be a huge honour to her.

Checking his watch nervously, he felt a knot form in his stomach. Thoughts flooding his mind at once. *Maybe I should have settled on something less challenging, was ballet really the right route for my first show?*

"Shit, what the fuck have I gotten myself in to?" he said, shaking his head. Realising that his palms had become increasingly sweaty again, he rubbed them against his legs as he walked over to the table. A selection of snacks had been placed upon it for himself and his dancers. When he had entered the room earlier, he had also placed a hipflask filled with Grey Goose vodka, and a bottle of Merlot there. Knowing fine well he may need the courage the alcohol would bring later in the evening. Or now to be precise. He knew he needed something to calm his nerves. Lifting the flask, he pulled at the top and took a deep swig, swallowing as his face creased. He did not even take time to let it settle before he took a longer, deeper mouthful. Gulping as he dropped into the chair beside him.

Still sweaty, but slightly more relaxed he let out a sigh. He wondered if his date was on her way. Tara had always come on a little too strong. He had often found it a turn off, but her looks more than made up for the fact that she bored the shit out of him. Intellectually she was not at his level, but damn her body made up for it. He wanted her on his arm tonight if just to make him look better.

She had jumped at the chance when he had asked her. She had beamed a prize-winning smile and bounced on the spot, her tits almost bursting from the tight blouse she wore. They had definitely been on his pros when he had mentally compiled his list in asking her along for the event. Tits, curves to die for, and the fact that she could turn heads would make her utter bullshit conversation worth it for one night.

Taking another, smaller swig of his vodka Gregory pulled his phone from his pocket, screen lighting as his finger caught it. An array of messages popping up. Taras's name catching his eye.

On my way hot stuff. In a bit xoxo

Rolling his eyes, he idly scrolled through the other messages. He even found her texts frustrating. Hardly worth a response, he put his phone back in his pocket. With the last little swig, he put his flask down.

His stomach was warm and his nerves at ease for now. Leaning back in the chair he closed his eyes. Running his hands through his hair he could feel the soft lull of the alcohol take over him, calming his nerves. He had fifteen minutes till show time. He just needed a quick shirt change then he was good to go. Getting up he began walking towards his clean shirt when he heard a knock at the door. Quickly pulling off his old one, he gave himself a quick spray of deodorant and threw on his new shirt. Slowly buttoning it up he was in no rush to see who was at the door, after all, no one rushes the man behind the show!

Tara

Waiting impatiently for an answer, Tara plumped up her waist length blonde hair at the roots, pouting as she ran her fingers through her curls. She really wanted tonight to go perfectly. She had spared no expense in getting herself ready for the evening. She had picked out the sexiest black dress she could find. The satin clung tight against her curves, her breasts practically spilling out the front, but that was the look she was going for. She'd had an interest in Gregory for months now. Working for the same company, albeit different departments, she had spotted the man one morning. She had been on the phone as he had entered her department. His tall athletic appearance catching her eye instantly. She had hoped to catch his attention, but he had not even looked in her direction. The man had sauntered past and into the office of her boss, without even a knock. It was then that she had realised his importance to the company, driving on her attraction even more.

Looking around suspiciously, aware of how eerie their chosen meeting place appeared at night Tara glanced back at her Ford Puma lonely in its spot in the desolate car park. Aware of the cold breeze enveloping her, she wondered if she was wasting her time. No response to her text and no answer now it appeared. She considered heading back to her car when suddenly the door to the building flew open. Gregory stood, smiling brightly.

"Tara!" he beamed. "So glad you could make it!"

"Gregory! Hi! I'm honoured that you chose to invite me to be your date," she said, looking up at him with a flutter of her lashes. She was feeling pretty confident that this night could end well for the both of them. She knew she looked phenomenal.

"So, am I driving or are you parked elsewhere?" she queried, gesturing towards the carpark behind her. Confusion crossing the man's features for a moment.

"No Tara, come in," he spoke, stepping to the side. "Did I not elaborate?"

Tara stepped into the room slowly, glancing around. She could see that she was in some kind of dressing room, looking at him as she passed, she could see he was grinning again.

"I actually hired this building. It's a community centre. Perfect for such an occasion. They have the stage, the lighting…and the main room is huge! I know Swan Lake is such an iconic performance, but I needed to be close to home. My mum you see, she's in ill health. So ideally, I needed to be near to her."

Feeling disappointment creeping in, Tara hoped that her face hid it. She had wanted glitz and glamour. Looking back at the man again she tried to give him one of her prize-winning smiles.

"I mean, I know it's no Opera House, but I was hoping for a more intimate evening. We don't need hundreds watching, just those closest to me."

Spinning around she rested her bum against the edge of the table behind her, hands behind her, knowing fine well it made her breasts stand to attention. It was one of her go-to moves to catch a man's eye. "So, Gregory. Has everyone arrived? Just the car park was empty?"

"Tara my dear, there's plenty of parking to the side and front of the building. I sent you around the back so we could watch the show together."

He spoke slowly, closing the gap between himself and the woman. Never taking his eyes from hers as he spoke. She flustered as he drew nearer, suddenly feeling nervous. He stood before her, reaching out. She flinched as he touched her arm, running his fingers down it. Still his eyes never leaving hers.

"You look stunning Tara. I definitely chose the right woman to be on my arm." He said, before gesturing to the table behind her, "Merlot? I brought a bottle for a pre-show drink to calm the nerves."

"I would love to Gregory. Just one though, yeah? Wine goes straight to my head," she giggled as she stepped to the side to allow him to prepare the drinks.

"Just one, I promise," he said, picking up the bottle and unscrewing the cap. "Unfortunately, we only have these plastic cups, but hey wine is wine, right."

Chuckling, she gave a nod of her head. Despite the fact he was obviously nervous, he still had that smouldering charm she found so enticing and he looked amazing in his suit. She could not help but bite the corner of her bottom lip as she watched him.

"Before we share a drink, I must use the bathroom, can you direct me?" she asked, knowing fine well she did not need to go, she just wanted to make sure she was up to standard.

"Straight out the door and it's the first one to your left, you can't miss it," he mumbled, without turning around.

Nodding with a smile, she headed to the door. Opening it up she saw a long dark corridor before her. Grateful that the bathroom was close, she began to walk forward. As the door behind her closed the light illuminating the corridor disappeared. Straining to see in the dark she spotted the faint outline of the doorframe ahead as her fingers grazed the wall she quickened her pace, the only sound to be heard was her heels clicking as she power walked her way forward. Opening the door, she was grateful to see the light automatically turn on. Stepping in she glanced around, the smell of stale urine hitting instantly. Grimacing she spotted the mirror and headed towards it. Slipping her bag from her shoulder she looked at her reflection. Pleased with what she saw, she knew he would be putty in her hands by the end of the night. Retrieving her lipstick from her bag she traced it over her lips before rubbing them together and checking her teeth for runaway red marks. Giving herself a final once over and a nod of approval to her reflection self, she turned on her heel and headed back to the door. As she opened the door to exit the bathroom, she peeked out cautiously, keeping her eyes on the entrance back to the Dressing room. Racing forward in her five-inch heels, she made it to the door in seconds. Opening it quickly, she slid in to see Gregory stood with a plastic cup of wine in each hand. Taking her drink, she thanked him.

"Cheers!" he said, holding his cup out.

"Cheers Gregory!" she declared, raising her drink to meet his. They drank in unison. Both seeming to drink a couple of seconds longer than the usual cheers, but she figured they both needed it.

"Five minutes till Show Time!" he announced, looking down at his watch. Wringing his hands together, clearly nervous of the impending performance, he spoke. "For years I've been waiting for this moment. I really hope I portray the true beauty of the performance."

Stepping forward, she took his hand in hers and she could feel how wet his palm was. Fighting not to flinch away she smiled warmly back at him.

"The performance will be amazing. Stop doubting yourself!" she quipped, swinging their hands as if they were two childhood friends about to go skipping down the road. "Now let's drink up and enjoy the night ahead."

Smiling back at her he seemed to ease slightly. She felt his fingers relax, relieved as he let go of her hand, she gave it a discreet wipe on the back of her dress as he took a long swig of his drink. Checking his watch again he spoke.

"Right, drink up beautiful, it's almost time!"

Finishing off the rest of his wine, he walked over to the mirror. She watched, smiling to herself. It impressed her that he seemed to take pride in his appearance. Watching him in silence, taking small sips as she did so till she had drained the cup. Tara placed her cup down on the table.

"Ready!" She said, suddenly feeling the warm buzz of the wine creeping in. Looking back at Gregory, she could see that he had already opened the door to the darkened corridor.

"After you." gesturing with his hand.

Alcohol easing her nerves, Tara sauntered over to the man, eyeing him with a seductive smile as she passed him. Relief washed over her as a light above flicked on. Seeing that Gregory had hit the switch, she gave him a warm smile and linked her arm with his. As they walked together in silence, she leant into him. Realising that the wine had hit her quicker than expected.

Damn drinking on an empty stomach! she thought to herself. Surprise hit her when he put his arm around her, guiding the young woman as they walked. She felt safe as she rested her head against his shoulder.

As they came to a door, he stopped suddenly, taking her hands as he pulled her to face him. She could see fear etched across the man's features. He seemed so vulnerable to her in the moment.

"Are you ready?" he said in a hushed tone, anxiety evident as his voice shook.

"I am Gregory, are you?" she purred. Looking into his dark brown eyes.

"Yes, let's do this." he squeezed her hands, letting go of one to open the door. Before her stood a large dimly lit room filled with chairs, although the room appeared to lack people to fill them. Suddenly, limbs feeling heavy, it took Tara a moment to shift herself into the room. She was confused. *Were people still waiting outside?* She felt his hand rest against her back and gentle ease her further into the room.

"Come on. Let's get you sat down. I thought mum would be here already, but it seems she is being her usual dramatically late self." he chuckled at his own comment. Still looking around, Tara let him lead her forward. Guiding her to the front row seats.

"Where is everyone?" she murmured, eye lids suddenly feeling heavy. Her vision blurring slightly. Blinking hard, she let him ease her down into a seat. Relieved as she leant back, realising how comfortable it was. Looking up she saw him smiling at her, his eyes bright. He seemed to buzz with excitement. Again, she spoke, slower than before. "Why are no other guests here yet?"

His smile never faltered. "I must go for a moment Tara dear. I fear mum must be running late."

He looked to the door at the far end of the room, "Give me a minute. I'll go check if she is waiting outside."

He caught her off guard as he cupped her cheek with his hand. "You really do look beautiful tonight; do you know that?"

Giving him a tired smile, she felt unable to form the words to respond so gave the man a slow nod.

As he departed, she did not even feel the need to watch him leave. Resting her head against the chair, she let her eyes scan the large stage before her. Even in the dull light she could tell that the solid wood was in need of a good varnish. A large burgundy velvet set of curtains hung atop it. Scanning the room before her she could see it was in dire need of a paint. She noticed patches of damp and large flakes of paint curling away from the wall. Cringing she began to wonder what she had let herself in for. *What kind of ballet show could be performed in a run-down old community centre?*

Upon hearing the click of the door behind her she was unable to muster the energy to look around. Tara knew she should not be feeling the way she was after just one large glass of wine, hell, one bottle could not even have this effect.

Hearing footsteps drawing closer she tensed. Closing her eyes for another prolonged blink, when she opened them, she saw that Gregory was stood before her again, hands atop his mother's shoulders as she sat in front of him in a wheelchair. The lady was dressed top to toe in white lace. Her shoulders were modestly covered in a lace shawl, while resting in her tightly wound grey bun, stood two large white feathers. The elderly lady made no attempt to speak, instead choosing to look away from the young woman.

"Well look who I found waiting outside." Smiling, Gregory gently squeezed his mother's shoulder. "Tara, I fear that Merlot may have gone to your head. You're looking a little worse for wear."

Concern washing over the man's features, he approached and kneeled before the woman, leaning in as he rested a hand on her knee. Again, unable to form the words, she merely smiled. *Could he have added something to my drink when I left the room?* Panic began to creep over her. Trying to lean forward she realised that she could not even muster up the energy to move.

"You just relax beautiful. I will get mum to her seat and get the show on the road…as they say. Then be back to watch the performance with my two very special guests for the evening." giving her hand a squeeze as he stood up, Taras eyes followed the man as he walked back towards his mother, guiding her wheelchair to the central aisle, one seat away from where he had placed Tara. From the corner of her eye, she saw him lean before the old lady, his hands placed lovingly against her cheeks as he spoke to her. Tara, unable to hear the exchange, looked on as he gently kissed his mother on her forehead. With one last glance at the two women, he gave each of them a nod, and headed towards the stage.

Once he was out of sight Tara looked back at his mother. Curious as to why the lady had not attempted to address her.

Had she not realised that something strange was going on?

Why had he brought her here?

She had expected a night of glamour, not a drugged up private showing in a shit hole community centre.

What the fuck?!

Suddenly the lights went out and darkness enveloped the room. Tara attempted to scream but was only able to let out a low moan, her eyes desperately searched for any form of light. Hearing the sudden sound of scraping metal, squinting, she realised she was able to see the huge curtains slowly begin to open. Behind them came the faintest flash of light, enough so that the woman could see the performers silhouettes. They stood, perfectly still. Seven of them, side by side.

With a sudden flash of light, the stage was lit by a spotlight from behind the young woman and almost instantaneously a speaker before the stage burst into life, Tchaikovsky's Swan Theme began to play loudly. With the addition of light, Tara could now see the ballerinas. Unable to move but only watch the performance before her. Low moans escaped her throat as she witnessed the sight before her. What at first, the young woman had assumed to be dancers, now appeared to be puppets. Terribly applied make up caked to the faces. Their limbs flailed aimlessly, with no rhythm, seemingly controlled by the large contraption that stood above the stage. Ropes coming down, secured around the dancers in different places, holding them in position. There was no grace to the performance. Looking closer Tara noticed that one of the puppets had what appeared to be blood, coming from its nose. Narrowing her eyes to get a closer look, Tara realised that it was an actual woman.

Was she unconscious or worse?

Scanning the other dancers as they jolted and jerked atop the stage, she realised that each one was an actual lady, but at different stages of decay. She felt her bladder loosen. Tara knew she had to get out, and fast. Trying with all her might, she pushed and forced herself to move but it was impossible, she was trapped in the shell that even she could no longer rely on. Internally screaming she scanned the room quickly. Looking for anything she could use, or a means of escape when suddenly she saw him, stood to the side of the stage. Standing in awe at the macabre performance before him. Instead of disgust and horror he appeared to be filled with love. As if sensing her watching him, he turned to face her, smiling practically from ear to ear. With a jump of excitement, he began to jog back to where Tara was.

Oh my God! His mother!

Straining to see the elderly lady, eyes wide, she desperately tried to focus on her, but he placed himself down into the seat between the two women. Gripping Taras hand, he squeezed hard. As much as she wanted to pull hers away from under his crushing grasp, she was unable to do so. *This is it; this is how I'm going to fucking die!* She thought to herself. Feeling a single tear run down her right cheek. She felt utter despair. *Why the fuck wasn't his mother trying to do something?*

Suddenly the man let go of her hand, placing his finger to her cheek to catch her lone tear. A look of surprise on his face.

"Tara!" he exclaimed, looking from his finger to her face. "Do you find so much beauty in the performance that you feel the need to weep?" He threw himself to her then, wrapping her in his arms and pulling her towards him. Her head and limbs falling as he embraced her. "Thank you so much Tara! Thank you! It means so much to me that you and mum enjoy the show!"

As he placed her back into her seat, head back so she could take in more of the performance she noticed the man turn away. Over the almost unbearably loud music, she could hear the faint mumbling of him talking to his mother.

Her eyes were drawn back to the stage. Mind racing, she feared where the night would lead. She had no way of getting out right now. She knew he was going to kill her. Why show her all of this just to set her free? Would she end up a swan just like those poor unfortunate dancers. *How had he gotten each of them?* The bloody nosed swan was obviously his newest addition, but some had obviously been dead far longer. One of the dancer's skin had begun to slip down her legs, revealing bone beneath. Another bloated, purple patches adorning her flesh. Fluid flicking off her hands and feet as her arms and legs flung and jerked. Feeling the nausea begin to rise she forced her eyes closed. She could not look any longer at the sight before her. *Those poor women!*

Suddenly she felt his fingers, prising at her eyelids, his voice now firm, shocking the young woman into opening her eyes.

"No! you can't go to sleep. Look at my beautiful dancers! So graceful. My Seven Swans a-Swimming.... Seven Swans a-Swimming." His eyes now glazed as he looked at his morbid creation with what she could only surmise as adoration.

With a jolt, the man spun around to face his mother. Tara could only see the back of him, but she saw him stiffen. With a sliver of hope, the woman wondered what had been said to cause him to react so suddenly. Straining to hear over the music she heard a shrill whine. He was suddenly on his feet, fists firmly at his sides as he now stood before his mother. Squinting to see the exchange she caught a glimpse of the elderly lady. Her skin shrivelled and brown. Deep holes lay where her eyes should have been. Her nose had long gone, now a dark cavity in its place. A gaping hole on her cheek revealing part of her jawbone, one lone tooth to be seen. Taras breathing quickened. The old woman had clearly been dead for years. Her body slowly decaying. While Gregory spoke to her, even kissed her!

What the fuck!!!!

She knew now that there was not an ounce of sanity left in the man. Suddenly she was brought back from her thoughts as Gregory screamed at the mummified corpse of his mother.

Gregory

"Are you fucking serious?!" The words escaping the man. Shame and regret hitting him instantly at his disrespect towards his mother. "You love swans mum!"

"I have never seen something so absurd in all my life Gregory James Hume. I mean look at those whores! What the fuck are they wearing?" The old woman turned to look at her son. Disgust upon her wrinkled features.

"I don't even fucking like Ballet! I don't think your little tart does either." she croaked loudly, raising a claw like finger to the young woman. "Can't even crack a smile."

She let out a cackle, turning back to her son.

His mum's words hit him like a kick to the gut. He had only wanted to show his devotion to her, and here she was, embarrassing him in front of his date. Looking back to the stage, he saw his dancers continued to perform, tears filled his eyes. They moved with grace, yet his mother spat out such vile words. Observing Tara, he could see that she was staring in confusion at he and his mum. The old woman continued to rant.

"I mean come on Gregory, I have more poise and grace taking a shit than those dancers do!" She chuckled to herself as she observed them. Gregory felt defeated. All his time and effort wasted. It had taken him such a long time to find his perfect performers, and all for it to be ridiculed by the woman he loved the most. Falling back into his seat, he turned his gaze to Tara. She was staring at the man, her head had fallen to the side, or had she moved it?

Maybe I should have used more medication? he thought to himself. Running his fingers down her arm he felt her flinch beneath his fingers.   a sign, he looked back at the stage. Even if his mum was going to ridicule the show, he was there to enjoy it. His seven swans moved with such beauty. Feeling the tears flow, he felt no shame. He was lost in the moment, observing the magic he had created. He knew he would have to try harder next time though. He had to be able to put a smile on the old bitches face somehow.

Suddenly pulled from his thought by his old mother's cackle, he turned to face her. Hand raised again, pointing to the stage, she laughed gleefully.

"Fucking hell son! She's lost an arm!" She continued to giggle as she bounced up and down in her wheelchair. Looking to the stage in confusing he could see it now. The rotted arm on the floor beside his ballerina. She kept moving but he could see her beginning to slip from the contraption that held his ballerinas. He had made it himself, another proud creation of his. The man needed something to make his women move. With a hard, wet smack, his dancer hit the floor, teeth scattering as she landed.

The sudden sound of retching drew the man's attention to his left. Vomit began to flow from the blonde woman's mouth, running onto her large breasts, and dress. With exceptional speed, Gregory shot up in front of the woman and placed both hands over her nose and mouth. Disgust hitting him as he felt the puke hit his palms, but it did not deter him. As he looked down at Tara, her eyes wide, he could hear her gargling from beneath his hands. Little sprays of vomit flying out as she coughed and spluttered. No strength in her to fight the man.

"Well Tara Baby! Why waste such a good night!"

Her eyes rolling, the woman's movements began to slow as she choked on her own vomit. Leaning in, he gave the young woman a kiss to the forehead before stepping back, letting her slump to the side as he admired her. He knew he had made the perfect choice.

"Don't worry beautiful, we will clean you up." He said softly, running his fingers through the deceased woman's hair. "Then we've work to do."

Looking back at his other performers, the man let out a deep breath, before looking back at the beauty before him.

"On to bigger and better things Tara! I plan to make you into my finest performer yet!"

Mother's Milk
Eric Butler

Winnie sat by the window and watched the rain fall. She cradled her newborn son to her breast and pressed her nipple to his lips. The baby latched on and began to suckle. Lightning flashed through the sky and illuminated the forest surrounding the old stone abbey. From her seat, she could just see the lonely road that weaved through the trees and up the hill to the building's giant gate.

Thunder boomed overhead, rattling the windows, and causing the baby to flinch. Winnie glanced down and shifted a bit to encourage him to start back up.

"It's okay, Peter," she whispered. "Nothing to be frightened of here."

"Seems like he's eating better," a deep voice said from the doorway.

Winnie shifted the blanket to cover herself. She didn't like it when Father Dullin appeared unannounced, and even less when her breast was exposed. There was something lurking behind his eyes that made her skin crawl. She looked up and forced a smile to her lips.

"Yes Father, he's really starting to get the hang of it," she said, trying to keep her voice light as the man stepped closer.

"Good … good," he said, his eyes locked on the boy. "I'm making my nightly rounds to see how everyone was doing before I head to bed myself."

"We're fine," she murmured, stifling a yawn with the back of her hand. "Just tired."

"That's expected. It's only been six days since you've given birth and Peter isn't tiny. That's why we have the wet nurses; to help you shoulder the strain while you recover."

"Yes Father," she replied. "But, I wanted to try."

"Commendable," he said, a smirk forming on his lips. "Just don't overdo it. Sister Agnes is coming up soon with your nutrients. I'll make sure she brings Joan with her."

Winnie grimaced at the mention of the green liquid the Sisters had been giving her since she arrived at the abbey but tried to play it off like another yawn.

"Well, you're tired and I still need to visit with the Sisters," he said, lingering a moment too long before turning to leave. At the doorway, he glanced back. "I hope you realize that you two are a blessing."

Winnie nodded, slowly at first, but more emphatically when she thought he might turn once again to engage. His smile widened, and he slipped out the door, pulling it closed behind him. She released a shuddered breath, relieved to be free from his attention. She tried to ignore the sudden pang of guilt she had at the thought, but her cheeks flushed in embarrassment.

Father Dullin had found her on the street, pregnant with nowhere to go, and given them a home here at the abbey. Who knew what might have happened to them if not for him. Gentle snores came from beneath the blanket across her chest. She pulled Peter free from her breast and kissed him on the forehead.

Nine months ago, she wouldn't have ever expected to love anything as much as she loved this tiny baby.

A blessing from God … on Christmas, no less.

***

Winnie stared at the glass of thick green liquid held out by Sister Agnes. She thought they would stop once the baby arrived, but then they started bringing it twice a day. She grabbed the glass with a sigh, pinched her nose, and began to drink. She swallowed repeatedly, trying to get the thick liquid down before she needed to take a breath.

"Ugh, what does this do again?" she asked, holding out the glass to show she was finished.

Sister Agnes took it and smiled. "Why it helps build up your immunity. Which you pass on to your baby through your milk, so he'll grow up big and strong."

"If the taste doesn't kill me first," Winnie replied, a sour look on her face. "Seriously, it's like you put a fish in a blender and tried to hide it by adding one of those pine air fresheners."

"That's how you know it's good for you," Sister Agnes said with a grin. "You look tired dear. Why don't you get some rest, and I'll have Sister Vera come and check on Peter in a bit."

"It's all this rain," Winnie mumbled, letting the Sister lead her to the bed and tuck her in.

"One more day, and I promise the rain will end," Sister Agnes said, sweeping Winnie's hair from her forehead with her fingertips. "After tomorrow, it will be a new year. A new beginning."

She turned off the light and slipped out of the room. Lightning flashed outside her window, and her baby stirred in the bassinet across the room. Winnie thought about getting up to check on him, but she was so tired. Thunder rumbled overhead, and the steady drum of the rain soon lulled her to sleep.

***

Father Charles Willfred couldn't sleep and reached over to turn on the lamp by his bed. He grabbed his watch and checked the time. *3:35.* He couldn't remember the last time he slept through the night. *At least not since being banished to The Domus Divinae Revelationis.*

"What a joke," he grumbled, unsure if he was talking about the abbey's name or himself.

He slipped out of bed and got dressed. *Some fresh air will help.* He nodded at the thought, letting himself buy into the lie. He stepped out of his room and walked down the long hallway to get to the cloister. That way he could walk around the garden and stay dry.

The hallway lit up for a second, and a crack of thunder echoed through the abbey. *Does it ever stop raining here?* He reached into his coat pocket and pulled out a flask. He glanced around, then shook his head in exasperation. Who could possibly be around to see him sneak a drink? Father Dullin and his odd gaggle of nuns, or the mother they kept stashed away?

He shrugged and took a long drink. He closed his eyes and savored the warmth as it travelled down to his belly. Once, he found that feeling within the church, but no longer. A sense of loss washed over him, and a single tear slipped from the corner of his eye and ran down his cheek. Thunder boomed overhead, and the rain started coming down harder. He opened his eyes and took another pull before slipping it back into his pocket. *Why am I here, Lord?* He tilted his head, but when no answer came, he wasn't surprised. God stopped talking to him years ago.

Father Willfred pushed open the door and shivered at the blast of cold air that rushed towards him. He stepped out onto the walkway and coughed when he took a deep breath. He cleared his throat and began walking forward. He focused on the steady drum of rain on the metal cover above, and soon his mind was clear.

The path itself formed a rectangle around a pleasant enough garden. It wasn't much to look at in December, but he was curious to see what spring would make of it. He came to the end of the walkway and turned right. Lightning streaked above, and for a moment, everything seemed frozen in time. *Is that Father Dullin?*

He leaned forward, trying to make out the figure through the downpour before it disappeared through the dormitory door. *Is this my ticket out of here?* Father

Willfred sprang forward and rushed through the rain, taking the quickest way to the opposite side of the garden. He slid to a stop at the door, pulled it open a crack, and saw the figure disappear around a corner.

Father Willfred stepped inside and crept forward. Low murmurs echoed through the room, and he struggled to make out what was being said. There was a soothing quality to the sound, and as he moved closer, he thought it might be Aramaic, but he wasn't sure. Languages were never his strong suit. He came to the spot where he last saw the figure and leaned forward enough to peek. His breath caught at what he saw.

In the center of the room, slightly suspended above a tub, sat an ovoid mass of flesh, reddish grey in color, and covered in writhing tentacles. Across the blob, random mouths opened and closed, and a low hum came from the mass, but he couldn't tell exactly from where. The abbey's eight nuns stood around the creature; their hands locked together to form a loose circle.

Father Willfred's heart began to pound, and his eyes grew wider. The Sisters, still chanting, stepped closer to the blob, and broke hands with each other to lay them on the pulsating flesh. Its tentacles wrapped around the women, and they began to massage the creature. After a few minutes, the hum grew in volume, and a thick green liquid oozed from its pours and dripped into the tub. The sound reminded him of vomiting, and he struggled to stop himself from retching. The women continued to knead the creature's flesh, and the liquid began to gush.

"This is not for your eyes, Blasphemer," Father Dullin hissed from behind and slammed a metal rod against the back of Father Willfred's head.

***

Winnie opened her eyes, and a sudden unease settled upon her. A scraping sound pulled her attention to the far wall, and after a moment, she realized it was slowly opening. A soft white light spilled into the room and backlit a figure. It stood there for a heartbeat, and then stepped into the room. She wanted to call out, to scream for help, but instead she simply lay there, frozen.

The figure seemed to glide across the room, and once it passed into the darker shadows, shifted from a human into a more shapeless blob. Six long tentacles squiggled out from the form, twitching and gyrating. Icy fear seized her heart, and goosebumps popped up on her skin as she followed the creature with wide unblinking eyes as it moved towards her baby's bassinet.

Oh God … No! She let the thought echo through her head, hoping it would somehow find its way to her lips. The thing stopped at the edge of the bassinet. Moist smacking noises came from the darkness, and she felt her bladder release. The tentacles wriggled over the lip and disappeared into the cradle. Winnie could feel the urine soaking through her pajamas and into the mattress below her. A sharp cry came from Peter, and lightning streaked outside her bedroom window. In that moment, she found herself staring at an unimaginable creature frozen in the sudden burst of light.

It was a pulsating mass of skin, covered with random eyeballs and tiny mouths, opening and closing as if they were suckling. Four of the tenacles supported the blob, holding it up so it could reach into the baby's bed. The light faded, and Bree struggled to see anything until her eyes readjusted. The tentacles lifted, and her baby cried again.

"*Soon,*" an impossibly deep voice whispered. "*You will be reborn ...*"

A crack of thunder rattled the window, and Winnie woke with a start. She pressed her hand against her chest and struggled to catch her breath. There was no one by the bassinette and her nightmare began to fade. She cringed when more thunder rumbled above the abbey, sure it would wake Peter. Sitting up, she waited for his cry, but nothing came.

"Whatever is the matter, child?" a voice asked from the darkness. Winnie shrieked, and the light by her bed clicked on. Sister Agnes looked down at her with concern in her eyes. "It's just me. I've brought your morning nutrients."

Winnie stared at the woman, her breaths coming in gasps as she tried to calm down. She pointed towards Peter, and Sister Agnes moved over to the bassinette. She reached down and picked up the baby and carried him to his mother. Winnie hugged him to her chest, and he grumbled but stayed asleep.

"Oh, dear," the Sister said, her lips shifting into a comforting smile. "It looks like you've had an accident. Let me go get Sister Ella and we'll get you all cleaned up."

She placed the glass on the table and reached over to brush Winnie's sweat-soaked hair from her forehead. "Your baby's going to need you healthy and strong, so drink up."

***

Father Dullin walked into Winnie's room holding a serving tray. "Sister Agnes told me you had a nightmare this morning, and since it's New Year's Eve, I've brought you a special treat."

He carried it over to where she sat by the window and placed it on her lap. She stared at it, and he pulled the cover off with a flourish. She glanced down and clapped her hands in excitement. There was a thick slice of chocolate cake and a tall glass of milk. She couldn't remember the last time she'd been allowed to eat anything deemed unhealthy, and she grabbed the fork before he changed his mind.

Father Dullin laughed and stepped closer to the window. He glanced over his shoulder and watched her take her first bite. "Looks like the rain is stopping."

"Yes, the day keeps getting better and better," she replied around a mouthful of cake. She wanted to slow down and savor it, but she continued to shovel bite after bite into her mouth.

Father Dullin moved over to the bassinette and reached in to rest his hand on Peter's chest. "You are the one chosen to be reborn."

Winnie's head jerked over, and cake crumbled from her opened mouth. "What did you say?" she asked, the words muffled.

"Hmm?" he replied, turning his head to lock eyes with her. He was still smiling, and he tilted his head a bit to the side. "Oh, nothing important. I'm sure Sister Agnes will be here soon with your nutrients, so eat up. And we can talk tomorrow."

He glanced back at Peter and stared at the boy for a few heartbeats before turning and walking out of the room. She waited until the door closed, and then spit the suddenly rancid tasting cake from her mouth onto the plate. Her stomach rolled, and she worried that she might vomit up the bit she already ate. She drank a little of the milk, and, after placing the tray on the floor, walked over to check on Peter.

He stared up at her with wide eyes and began to open and close his mouth. She reached down and scooped him up. "Is it time for dinner, Peter?" she asked, settling back into the chair. She sighed when he latched on, and watched the sun slowly set through her bedroom window.

***

Winnie opened her eyes just in time to see the opening in the wall slide shut. Moonlight shined through the window, and she turned her attention to the bassinet. Nothing looked amiss, but a sudden spike of fear stole her breath. She threw back the covers and scrambled from her bed. She hissed when her bare feet touched the ice-cold floor but didn't stop to find her slippers, and instead rushed to Peter's crib.

"Where is he?" she wailed, staring down at the empty bassinet.

Winnie ran to the door and grabbed the knob only to find it locked. Crying for help, she repeatedly slammed her fist against the door until her hand ached. She backed away, now realizing no one was coming to check on her. They had what they wanted.

She rushed to her bedside, turned on the light, and found her slippers.

After she angled the lampshade to shine more light on the wall, Winnie stepped over to investigate it. Running her hands over the rough stone, she was about to give up hope, when her middle finger brushed over a smooth spot. She pressed down and after a moment, there was an audible click and the hiss of stone sliding against stone.

Winnie stared at the dark opening, and after a brief hesitation, stepped into the hidden passage. A flash of light grabbed her attention, and she shuffled through the darkness in that direction. She held her arms out and moved slowly so as not to run into anything. Each step seemed to drag into minutes, and soon, it felt like she'd been trapped in the dark for an eternity.

She struggled to catch her breath, each one coming as a strangled gasp. Her chest grew tight, and she wondered if the pounding she heard was her heartbeat. Up ahead, a beam of light shined through the wall. Winnie lurched forward, desperate to discover where the light came from. Her foot caught the edge of a stone block, and she tumbled to her knees with a gasp.

Wincing, she bit her bottom lip and tried to stifle the groan building in her chest. Muffled voices drifted into the passageway, and after breathing in and out through her nose to fight through the pain, Winnie crawled towards the light. She realized she was at another secret doorway that had not closed all the way. She pressed her eye to the opening and her breath caught. *What in God's name is that?*

A large pulsating blob of flesh sat suspended over a metal tub. Her eyes grew wider when they fell upon the nude man bound beneath the thing. The eight nuns stood spaced out around it. To the right, stood Father Dullin and beside him on an altar lay Peter, bundled in a folded strip of muslin. The priest stepped forward.

Winnie struggled to her feet and tried to pull at the opening to make it wide enough for her to slip through. The Sisters' voices grew louder, and Father Dullin reached into his robe and pulled out a knife with a black, crooked blade. He held it high above the pulsating mass and right when the nuns grew quiet, drove it down into the creature. There was a wordless howl, and its tentacles lashed about while it quivered and throbbed. Father Dullin pulled the blade free and began to repeatedly stab at the thing.

Gooey yellow pus spilled from the wounds and sloshed down on the man laying in the tub. His eyes shot open, and he began to scream, his shrieks of agony melding with the creature's lament as his flesh began to smolder and melt. The priest slashed the blade across the thing's flesh until it grew still. He stepped back to the altar and lifted Peter to cradle against his chest.

Father Dullin moved back to the unmoving mound of flesh, and the nuns threw their hands up, their fingers wriggling as if they might snatch the infant from his grasp. One final gurgle issued from the goopy mess in the tub, then the room fell into a quiet hush. The priest lifted Peter to his lips and kissed the baby softly on his forehead before laying him down inside the tub.

Winnie stopped struggling to open the door by force and began to look for the hidden mechanism. Movement pulled her attention back to the room, and she watched as the bottom of the thing's flesh quivered and throbbed. Her throat tightened as the skin stretched out until it tore, and a thick red worm began to wriggle out from the opening. It dangled above Peter for a moment and then slithered out to fall into the tub.

"Stop it," she pleaded, no longer worried if they knew she was there. "Don't let it near my baby."

Those in the room ignored her cries and instead watched with rapt attention as it squiggled closer to Peter. Father Dullin raised his arms towards the heavens, and the nuns began to repeat the word

Z'Yu'Gotha, each time louder than the last. Peter began to cry, and the worm slipped past the baby's lips and slithered into his mouth. The nuns grew quiet and leaned forward.

His cry morphed into a strangled choking whine, and then silence. Winnie slumped to the floor, and pressed her hands to her face, unable to watch anymore. Her sobs echoed through the darkness, and after a moment, the wall began to slide open.

"Rise, Sister Gwendolyn," Father Dullin said, holding out his hand to help her stand. "It is the Dawn of a New Age."

A baby's cry came from the room, and Winnie looked up. She let the priest guide her through the nuns that now crowded around the tub. She looked down and her breath caught. Laying in the yellow gloppy mess was a greyish pink blob. Tentacles wriggled out from the side, and tiny mouths with jagged little fangs made smacking sounds. Two eyelids fluttered open and large black eyes stared up at her.

Father Dullin pulled out the dagger and Sister Agnes took it from his hand. She turned and ran the blade across the throat of the nun closest to her. Blood gushed from the wound and the woman crumpled to the floor. Peter began to fuss, and his tentacle reached towards Winnie.

Father Dullin laid his hand on her shoulder. "It is time for you to join us. Your baby is hungry, and nothing is better for him than his mother's milk."

-The End-

Nine Ladies Dancing
Lee Richmond

Report on the trial of Alice Crane and the Crane sisters by Edmund Donovan.

Sunday - December 21st - 1608 AD
Yorkshire – England.

It all started with a pile of small bones.

There was I, Edmund Donovan; a Puritan clergyman named Geffron Hopkins, who had recently been appointed Witchfinder General; and a gaggle of local folk. We'd scoured the woods to the east of the town of Crowsholt, hoping to find some clue as to the whereabouts of the children that had gone missing over the last month. It had not gone well.

Sorrow and despair had spread through the town like a plague at a time when the locals should have been preparing to feast, drink, and gamble on dice and card games, as was customary this time of year. Whatever had taken the young ones cared naught for Christmas celebrations.

The first of the children to disappear had been the twins, Piers and Amelia, the son and daughter of the town doctor, Randolf Black. At first, the finger of suspicion had pointed squarely at the good doctor's wife, Rose. As anyone who knew her would attest, Rose Black was a strange character. She preferred to keep herself to herself, spurning the community and, therefore, maintaining an air of mystery. As is common in a town where everyone knows everyone else's business, mystery breeds mistrust. And so, tongues started to wag, gossip began to spread, and whispering voices passed unfounded accusations back and forth. That was until the disappearance of little Molly Cabot.

Molly had vanished on a Sunday afternoon while playing out in the snow-covered street while her parents enjoyed a drink at the Four Horsemen Inn. It would have proven impossible to blame Rose Black, as she and her husband sat drinking in the corner of the same gloomy inn that Molly's parents happened to frequent that very afternoon.

Between that Sunday and the evening of the discovery of the bones, thirteen more children had disappeared, and any semblance of joyful, festive spirit left the small community of Crowsholt.

Soon, words such as 'cult' and 'witchcraft' made their way into the whisperings, spurred on by the local clergy and parroted by the frightened townspeople, which is why I find myself working alongside Geffron Hopkins. I don't mind telling you I do not like this man. He is a bullish brute of a man, hellbent on punishing any woman he considers guilty of witchcraft, despite the possibility of there not being an ounce of truth to his accusations.

The gullible locals may have swallowed all that witch nonsense, but I never did. Even after meeting the Crane sisters, but I'll get to them soon enough.

Geffron Hopkins arrived in town four days before the discovery of the bones. In that short time, he'd managed to stir the locals into a frenzied mob that foamed at the mouth like a rabid dog. Now, I understand why it wouldn't have taken much effort to whip the grieving townspeople into a rage because their hearts had been shattered. I don't have children myself, but that doesn't mean I lack the capacity to empathise with these poor people. I just find the Witchfinder's methods to be underhand. A manipulative man can easily pull the strings of a group of people if they are frightened enough, and my people were plenty scared.

So, having created his army, we marched, mob-handed, into the woods, armed with axes, pitchforks, machetes and any other weapons that people could lay their vengeful hands on. I chose not to arm myself. Accidents happen, and I didn't wish to maim or kill someone because they might have stepped out of the shadows and taken me by surprise. I'm no pacifist, but nor do I want innocent blood on my hands.

As I stated earlier, eventually we entered a clearing, and that's when we made our grisly discovery. A pile of bones. Small bones that could only have belonged to children, stacked carefully so as to almost form a pyramid. A tiny skull topped the pyramid, like some ghastly treetop decoration. The light from the winter's moon bathed the skeletal remains as if some celestial being wished to highlight our macabre find. It was truly a horrific sight.

The bone pile was the beginning of this awful nightmare. More bones lay a couple of feet from the stack, only this time they had been arranged to form a five-pointed star. Circling the star were nine sets of footprints embedded in the snow that covered the clearing floor. The footprints were small, indicating they most likely belonged to women without a shoe's protection from the cold. All I could think at that moment was how anyone could stand to be outside in this weather without coverings of any kind to protect the naked foot from the frost. The prints in the powdery snow led away from the hellish boneyard, and Geffron Hopkins led the way, hoping to follow them to the guilty party before a fresh dusting of snow covered them over.

As luck would have it, the weather, in its infinite wisdom, was on our side. We followed the footprints through the woods, and as the temperature plummeted, we battled on, pulling our overcoats tight to our bodies in the vague hope of staying as warm as possible. We must have walked for hours before reaching the end of the treeline. Having never left Crowsholt, I had not the slightest clue as to where we had ended up.

The prints continued onward, and we pressed on, following them across an empty field before coming to a narrow river. We crossed the river using the same bridge as those who'd left the prints, and that's when we found the house.

I use the word house lightly as the building ahead of us was more of a wooden shack. Actually, if I had to compare, it resembled a barn that had been converted into a living space. Black smoke billowed from a crudely constructed chimney, and a light from somewhere within indicated that the ones we sought were most likely at home.

To my surprise, Hopkins walked up to the door and gently knocked. It was a friendly knock, the tap a cousin or brother might give when arriving to share supper. I half expected the man to hammer at the door with his fist or forgo a knock altogether and kick the door from its hinges. It seemed out of character that he did neither.

A shuffling of feet could be heard from inside, each step growing nearer and then a deadbolt sliding. I'm surprised I was as aware of the noises as I was, given that I could also hear my heartbeat as it pulsed and pounded in my ears. I'm not sure I remember why I was so anxious. I suppose it could have been that I was about to come face to face with the ugly visage of death that had murdered the children of the town I called home.

As the door was opened I and, I'm guessing, every member of the mob audibly gasped. It wasn't ugliness that greeted us from within. It was beauty. Before me stood the most beautiful woman I had ever laid eyes on, smiling the way I imagine angels smile. She stepped out into the night with an ethereal grace, and it's safe to assume there wasn't a man among us who wasn't enamoured.

Such was her exquisiteness that it took a while for anyone to realise that the woman's clothing, which was nothing more than a white nightgown, appeared to be caked in something resembling blood. Her face, neck and chest were covered in what looked like dried sanguine fluid. Still, we stood transfixed by her elegance and attractiveness. Well, almost all of us.

Whatever spell she had cast on the group seemed to have little to no effect on the Witchfinder. He was completely immune. Geffron Hopkins would later go on record stating that when the door opened, all he saw was a monster. But then, I can't help but feel that the misogynist within him regards all women as monsters. I had to wonder who the woman was who'd very clearly damaged this horrid little man.

The young woman wasn't alone. Eight equally stunning ladies followed out into the cold night air. Blood stained the clothing and, otherwise, flawless skin of each of them. They lined up, standing shoulder to shoulder before the stunned mob, a strange smile plastered on their beautiful faces.

Wednesday - December 24th - 1608 AD

The last few days have been terrible, to say the least. I have never witnessed such wanton cruelty in all my years as Clerk of the Court. This whole affair has shaken me to my very core.

The accused, Alice Crane, eldest sibling of the Crane sisters, admitted to the crimes the moment she was taken into custody. I see no reason for the torture and interrogation that has, so gleefully, been carried out by the clergyman Geffron Hopkins and his goonish lackeys.

She wasted no time confessing to the murders of the children, even going as far as detailing how the bones we had discovered in the neighbouring woods had been used as part of a satanic ritual. According to Ms Crane, she and her sisters had been travelling the land performing similar rituals for the last two-hundred and thirty-seven years. As she explained it, the ritual has been used to keep her 'coven', as she put it, young and healthy for the last two centuries. I have, on many an occasion, been accused of being a sceptic, but I prefer to think of myself as a sane and deeply rational person, and the ramblings of Alice Crane should be considered evidence for an insanity plea.

Unfortunately, if these things were to be simply dismissed as delusions due to the accused not being of sound mind, then we wouldn't have a church appointed Witchfinder General, would we?

Part of my duties as Clerk of the Court is to detail the interrogation used for establishing guilt, and this is the part that turns my stomach, especially when one considers the process to be completely unnecessary.

The first method Hopkins deemed appropriate was what is known as a swimming test. Believe me, the name sounds relatively benign, but the method is anything but.

Hopkins and his cronies dragged the Crane sisters to the bank of the Grenwell River and bound their hands and feet with rope. The nine women were then pushed into the icy waters. The idea behind this method is that if the women have spurned the sacrament of baptism, then the water will eject them, thus proving their allegiance to the devil himself. Of course, the women sank like stones.

Personally, I would have considered it a mercy to allow the Crane sisters to drown, but Hopkins had other ideas. Deciding that any form of death at this stage in the game would enable the women to get off far too easily, the Witchfinder ordered his men to jump in and pluck the women from the depths of the freezing river.

As the nine ladies lay shivering on the frost-covered ground, I couldn't help but feel that there wasn't an ounce of humanity left in the baying crowd who stood chanting callously at the accused.

I should make it known that I understand why the townsfolk were as angry as they were, and I'm not for one second trying to say that I don't believe these wicked women shouldn't be punished. But this was too much. I am a man who believes in the law, and I firmly believe that justice must be served; however, I am not a savage, and I find malicious intent for the sake of it to be truly revolting.

Later that same day, feeling that the Crane sisters hadn't suffered enough for one day, Hopkins called upon a handful of the townspeople to look for what he referred to as the 'Witches Mark'. This involved disrobing the accused and having what he called neutral adjudicators search the women's bodies for any sign that they were in league with Satan. When asked what they should be looking for, Hopkins told them to look for anything out of the ordinary, including moles, scars, birthmarks, and sores. Now, I don't think I know of a single person who doesn't have at least one of those things somewhere on their body, so, predictably, Hopkins was delighted when every one of the nine women was found to have some form of a blemish on their flesh. The whole process only confirmed, in my mind, what a farce this indeed was.

As I expected, those chosen to search the women's bodies were all male, and I had to leave the room when the overly zealous men began taking a little too much pleasure in the job at hand. It fills me with revulsion when I think of how ordinary people can be so abhorrent when there are no consequences. Geffron Hopkins stood watching, a creepy smile plastered on his face, as eager hands explored parts of the humiliated women's bodies they had no business exploring.

The eight younger Crane sisters sobbed as they were maltreated and caressed by the slathering pigs who felt it appropriate to violate their bodies with probing fingers, but not Alice Crane. She stood firm, her gaze locked on something far off in the distance. Something unseen by anyone but her. She seemed to have this air of belligerence about her, a bloody-minded attitude that refused to allow herself to be broken by anything these perverts did to her. As unnerving as it was, I couldn't help but admire her strength of spirit.

Once again, later that night, I questioned Hopkins on why he continued with this line of torture, considering that Alice Crane had already confessed to their crimes. The answer he gave chills my bones as I write this.

'Because I can.'

Thursday - December 25th - 1608 AD

It's Christmas day, the anniversary of the birth of our Lord Jesus Christ, and Geffron Hopkins has not spent the day resting with loved ones. His justification is that 'evil never takes a day off, so nor shall he.'

I believe it's more a case where there are no loved ones to spend time with. It's not hard to believe that no one wishes to spend a moment in the company of this bloated, malicious swine if they don't have to.

Still, the torture continues, and still, Alice Crane refuses to break. The eight other ladies have all eventually snapped. I in no way blame them. The cruelty they have been subjected to would subsequently break the hardiest of spirits.

Hopkins has been subjecting the women to something he calls the 'Pricking'. Pricking involves stabbing the women with hot needles. The belief was that sooner or later, the veil would slip, and the women would reveal that, with the devil's aid, the hot needles were causing no real pain or harm. Of course, this was absurd. The damage was perfectly evident, as every puncture wound inflicted on the women over the last few days had turned septic. As the infection spread, the nine ladies appeared quite sick. The youngest of the sisters, Arietta Crane, had turned a ghastly greyish-green colour and seemed to slip in and out of consciousness with alarming regularity. But still, Hopkins persisted with his methods.

I should note that from here on, I will be refraining from using the word 'interrogation'. This isn't an interrogation. It's torture, for torture's sake. Plain and simple. I have spent the last few days questioning my place in all this. I don't condone it, yet I am utterly powerless to prevent further suffering. I am the only sane, compassionate voice in a choir of madmen, and I am lost in the noise of the song.

This isn't God's work that is happening here. It is the work of men who claim to oppose evil yet act in a way that the devil himself would find shameful.

Where I once felt sympathy with the people of Crowsholt, I now feel contempt. This torture is allowed to continue because the townspeople demand it. This isn't justice. This is vengeance.

The ladies remain bound by chains that hang from the ceiling. Their arms are manacled above their heads as their bodies dangle weakly beneath, covered in their own feculence. Day and night, a constant stream of visitors arrive to beat or have their way with the women, ensuring that there is never a moment of rest or relief. Assault is not the work of the Lord.

The guilt eats me alive as I lay in bed each night, and the screams of these women fill my aching head, but I know there is nothing I can do to ease this suffering.

I sound like a coward.

I am a coward.

It will haunt me till the day I die.

As the saying goes, Christmas is a time of peace and goodwill to all men. I guess that doesn't include all women.

Tuesday - December 30th - 1608 AD

Hopkins has really unleashed his inner sadist over the last few days. Each of the nine Crane sisters has visited the rack.

In case you're unfamiliar, the rack is a wooden contraption fitted with chains. The victim is laid onto the barbaric device, and their arms and legs are strapped to a series of chains and pulleys. A handle is then gradually cranked, causing the victim's limbs to slowly stretch until they finally give under the pressure and dislocate at the knees, elbows, shoulders and any other such joint. It is a brutal mechanism, and I'm not too proud to admit that upon hearing the cracking and popping of joints, coupled with the wails it provoked, I excused myself to find a corner within which to vomit.

Once satisfied that the women had been subjected to enough suffering on the rack, Hopkins returned them to their cells, once again to be suspended with manacles that hung from the rafters above. I can't begin to imagine how it must feel to have your weight resting on dislocated limbs. Strangely, not so much as a whimper escaped any of the sisters as they were shackled. I can only assume they had somehow adapted to the relentless pain.

I had, by this point, seen enough. It was here that any professional relationship between myself and Geffron Hopkins dissolved into nothing short of unbridled disdain. I wasted no time in telling him how I found his methods inhumane and sadistic, and he wasted even less time in letting me know how he found me to be weak of stomach and an overpaid bureaucrat with no business sticking my nose into the affairs of the church.

It was those very words that convinced me to see this whole affair through to the end. I imagine it seems childish but knowing that my presence irked him so much superseded my desire to be as far away from this madness as humanly possible.

It is my intention to detail, as much as possible, the actions of this impotent troll of a man who not only seems to lack any semblance of compassion, empathy, or mercy but goes about his horrendous duties with a song in his heart and a smile on his face.

Geffron Hopkins is a psychopath in every sense of the word. A cold, ruthless, soulless man, masquerading his devilish orchestrations under the banner of God.

As I've already documented earlier in this report, the Crane sisters have never denied that they were responsible for the deaths of all these local children. They have also admitted that they did what they did as part of some satanic ceremony whereby they believe, quite remarkably, that the ritual somehow brings them eternal youth.

Do I believe these women need to be punished? Absolutely. Should that punishment mean a death sentence? Well, that is the law, and the law must be upheld. Is this needless torture necessary? No, of course, I don't believe it to be so.

We are all losing sight of what makes us good and righteous men.

Saturday - January 3rd - 1609 AD

Finally, the day of execution has arrived, and I feel an enormous sense of relief. Relief for myself because this whole ordeal has placed a permanent stain on my soul, and relief for the nine women who have found themselves at the mercy (or lack thereof) of the Witchfinder General.

There is a buzz of excitement about the town that would lead anyone not in the know to think we were hosting a carnival. I find the whole thing to be nothing short of macabre. I understand that for many, a sense of justice, maybe even closure, will be garnered from this evening's execution. I can only hope that those affected most by these women's crimes will find peace once this ordeal ends. But this party atmosphere leaves an acrid taste in my mouth and knots in my stomach. I have passed on having breakfast, for I fear that anything consumed will find its way back out again.

I stopped by to visit the Crane sisters before taking my morning walk. I'm still shocked that they have all survived to this day, given the poor conditions they have been subjected to and the infections that have ravaged their bodies.

Where once so beautiful, they now appear emaciated and withered, and their skin, which once glowed a gorgeous pink hue, is now a sickly greenish colour.

A priest was busying himself, reading the Crane's their last rites. I guess he thought their souls might still be worth saving. I hope he's right, but I doubt it. If God is watching over this, I doubt he is forgiving of the senseless murder of children. Then again, maybe he would consider that these ladies had suffered enough. The suffering inflicted upon them these past few weeks may serve as sufficient penance in his eyes.

Who am I to question the wisdom of God?

One day, we'll all be judged, and when Geffron Hopkins stands before our Lord, his fate might not be that different to that of the witches.

Let he who is without sin cast the first stone.

Hopkins has condemned the Crane sisters to death by fire. Nine stakes have been erected in the town square above nine bonfires. When announcing the method of execution, he claimed that the fire would cleanse the women's souls. I think the townsfolk swallowed his reasoning, but I think he just wants to see them burn. What a terrible way to leave this world.

Never let it be said that the residents of Crowsholt are ever shy to capitalise on an event. As I write this report, local businesses are setting up stalls in the square. Everyone from the greengrocer to the butcher to the baker has seized today as a moneymaking opportunity. There is even a cake stand. Is this standard practice for a witch burning? Are cake stalls a normal, everyday part of putting someone to death, or is this morbid attempt at cashing in a Crowsholt anomaly?

Any loss of human life, regardless of circumstance, should not be cause for celebration, much less a party. I hope that when this is over, the people of Crowsholt take time to reflect on their actions and do a little soul-searching. They might not like what they see when they look in the mirror.

I will wrap up my report tomorrow once the deed is done.

Sunday – January 4th – 1609 AD

This is to be my final entry reporting on the trial of the Crowsholt Witches. I also wish to use this entry to tend my resignation. After having spent the last fortnight privy to the most heinous undertakings, the likes of which no man should ever bear witness to, I can no longer in good conscience carry out my duties as Clerk of the Court effectively or impartially. I understand that this desire to forfeit my position might seem rash or ill-advised, but I owe it to myself not to be further embroiled in events that I find to be immoral.

I have never witnessed, nor should I wish to again, anything like the events of last night.

The sun set around five in the evening, which is around the time that crowds of locals gathered to witness the execution of the Crowsholt Witches. It was a particularly chilly evening, but many of the townspeople gathered without jackets. From what I gathered from the chatter, they expected to be warmed by the fires that were due to be lit.

The same priest I had witnessed reading the women's last rites stood before the crowd and gave a speech about how the lord condemned any person to be found in league with the devil and how we should find that same condemnation within ourselves. He then went on to preach about how, as God's children, we should reach inward and find forgiveness in our hearts because a lack of forgiveness leads us down a dark path of bitterness and resentment.

I found his sermon to be a cycle of contradictions and hot air. Which was it to be? Condemnation or forgiveness? Surely, you can't be about both. Nobody else seemed to pick up on the fact that the priest was tripping over his mixed beliefs.

Once the priest had finished, Geffron Hopkins took his place and began reading from a scroll he'd prepared. It didn't differ much from what the priest had said moments before, except there was no disingenuous mumbo-jumbo about forgiveness. The Witchfinder was not a forgiving man, and he cared nought for the sanctity of the souls of those he put to death.

On finishing his speech, Hopkins nodded to the jailer that it was time to bring out the condemned.

The women shuffled out into the town square, one after another, their hands bound behind their backs with rope. There they stood before the jeering crowd who had already begun throwing rotting fruit. The sound of cussing and name-calling was deafening. I couldn't help but feel saddened that the last thing these women would hear before suffering a horrific death would be such hatred and hostility.

The eight younger Crane sisters had begun weeping, the knowledge that this would be their final moments on God's green Earth becoming too much for them to accept. Alice Crane, however, never let so much as a murmur escape her. Her eyes burned with the same hatred as the crowd that stood before her. Her blank expression never faltered, even as she was led to the top of the pyre and tied to the stake that would hold her in place while she burned. She was a picture of eerie calm, and I found it quite unsettling.

Once bound to their stakes, Hopkins addressed the women, asking if they had any last words to impart before they met their maker. Some pleaded for mercy, others sobbed. Arietta Crane had already passed out, the infection that consumed her having almost finished her before a flame so much as licked at her feet. I prayed that she wouldn't awake to suffer any further torment.

The only one to open their mouth and speak was Alice Crane, who told the Witchfinder how she would wait for him in Hell. She followed her words with a large gob of saliva, which she spat directly into Hopkins' eye. I must admit that, while I don't condone this behaviour, it took a great deal of effort to keep a smile from my face.

Embarrassed and furious, Hopkins gave the order to proceed with what he called 'The Baptism of Fire'. A few of Hopkins lackeys stepped forward bearing torches and ignited the kindling at the bottom of each pyre.

Having never witnessed immolation before, I was somewhat surprised by how fast the fire took hold. In mere moments, the wood at the women's feet was consumed in fire, and that's when the sound that will be there with me every night when I close my eyes started.

I didn't know human beings were capable of making such a noise. I've read stories of Banshee's and often wondered what one might sound like if one were to encounter such a creature. I can only assume that it wouldn't hold a candle to the sounds that came from the Crane sisters last night.

The skin on the women's arms and legs had begun to blister and peel before the flames had so much as touched them. I, unfortunately, was close enough to see, with perfect clarity, the effect the heat was having. As their skin blackened and split, I thanked God that I had decided against eating that day.

Thankfully, the flames soon latched on to the Crane sister's frocks, masking the gorier details of their demise. The fire spread until the women were engulfed completely. Still, the shrieking continued as the witches writhed in agony. The rope that bound them to their stakes eventually surrendered to the flame, and as their bondage gave way, the women stumbled forward, their arms flailing wildly as they pirouetted in a panicked trance. Having become one with the inferno, they twirled and floundered with otherworldly grace. A burning nonet of radiant, swaying flame. It was both beautiful and horrifying in equal measure.

I prayed for the women to succumb to their injuries and for their suffering to come to an end, but it seemed endless. The screams, the flailing, and the smell, which will stay lodged in my nasal cavities till the day I die, went on for what seemed like an eternity.

Even the crowd, which had cheered so gleefully at the beginning, had become hushed. A stunned silence befell everyone in attendance, their mouths open and their complexions growing ever paler the longer it took the Cranes to perish.

Eventually, and thankfully, perish they did. Their burnt, lifeless husks fell and rolled through the burning pyre before coming to rest at the feet of the onlookers, who quickly backed away in disgust. Even the unflappable Geffron Hopkins appeared shocked by how long the Crane sisters had taken to depart this life.

Rather than hang around and risk questioning from the townspeople, the Witchfinder General made his excuses and vanished. That was the last Crowsholt saw of Hopkins. I can only assume he packed his things and departed before daybreak this morning.

As I stated earlier in this report, this is to be my final entry and, for that matter, my final report as Clerk of the Court. I can't shake the atrocities I have witnessed over the last few weeks. I feel they have negatively impacted me on so many levels. I have seen a side to human nature that I will never understand, nor do I want to.

And most importantly, I will never forget the sight of the nine ladies dancing.

Edmund Donovan
Clerk of the Court.

Ten Lords A Leaping
D.E McCluskey

1

The room was dark. There was a smell in the air that spoke of indulgence and privilege. It told tales of past family glories, it revelled in current successes, and generations of entitlement and nepotistic indulgence.

The walls were covered in fine mahogany panelling that sported portraits of important people from long ago, and some from not so long ago. Even the pictures spoke of smugness, the people caught within them exuding a heightened sense of self-worth and elitism that was no doubt undeserved.

This place had born kings, and prime ministers. It had facilitated the educations of lords, dukes, generals, even the odd field marshal had passed through this room. Wealthy landowners, and sycophants galore had paid many a pound, shilling, and pence to put their sons into this prestigious room.

The smell of fine wooden furniture polish filled the air, that was cleaned and buffered every day by underpaid cleaners, who were jeered and mocked, and sometimes physically abused if they had the misfortune to be running behind in their duties and been present when the boys returned from their classes.

The delightful smell of the polish had been pushed way down the pecking order tonight. This was Christmas Eve, the most special of nights in this institution. It was a night of wild abandon. It had been this way for time immemorial. It was the night when the boys would play at being men. A night where anything goes, and usually did.

The party usually started around four in the afternoon, in a few of the taverns around the town, before inevitably winding up in these revered chambers.

The polish had been bullied from the fore by the stink of spilled alcohol, mostly brandy, the expensive kind. Even this had been quashed by the stink of expensive cigar smoke, puffed once and coughed back out again. There was also the stink of greasy food, far too much food. It had been ordered, prepared, and left to go cold, and to waste, as another show of excess these boys didn't care about. There were people, families in the cold streets around this campus, shivering in the snow, their flesh freezing, their stomachs empty, and their throats dry. The food wasted in this common room would have been enough to sustain for them for weeks, yet up here, in this lavish, ivory tower, high over the good city of Oxford, these boys didn't care. They only cared about themselves, and about each other. Absolutely everyone else was there for them to crush beneath their boot heels.

There was one last stink that lay heavy in the room. This was a blend, and it was disgusting. It would have clogged the nostrils of any newcomer. However, these boys had gotten used to it, even revelled in it. They thought of it as the smell of their privilege. Merely by the good fortune of being born to exploitative families with dubious, and sometimes criminal backgrounds, they saw themselves as earning this stink.

It was the stench of life, and it was the reek of death.

The first part of the blend was hormonal sweat. The ten youths in the room were no more than fifteen years of age. Spotty, grubby, overweight, post pubescent boys. The heavy oozing of pheromones was offset with the stodgy, dull reek of their semen.

This would have been no different in any fifteen year old boy's chambers, but when ten of them were together, and after what they performed, as an initiation ceremony, and to reiterate their loyalty to their rotten club, but mostly just because they could; the hideousness was thick, heavy, and wet. If one had a large knife, they might have been able to cut a swathe through the cloying thickness of their semen.

The death smell was from the severed head of a pig that lay on one of the tables.

The poor beast had been butchered, not for its meat, that would, again, have fed many a starving family for weeks, but purely for their entertainment, and the time-honoured tradition of these boys pledging their allegiance to their filthy, elitist club.

The head lay in a puddle of pearlized gloop, that any mother would have recognised instantly, if they hadn't already from the smell. The poor beast's dead mouth hung open, with more of the abundant liquid dripping, oozing from it. Its glazed eyes were covered too, as was the rest of its cold, decaying flesh.

The Bullingdon Club's Christmas party had been in full swing.

But now the ten boys, filled with food, drink, and an arrogance they didn't deserve, lay on the plush, lavish couches. Some in a state of undress, others fully clothed, complete in dining suites and cloaks, yet all of them asleep. The sound of snoring reverberated around the room, as each slept the sleep that only the rich could afford. While others wrapped their meagre scraps of clothing around their children, in futile attempts to cull the cruel, cutting, and deadly December winds, the rich slept warm, without a care in the world.

~~~~

Although not everything in the lavish room was still. As the clock slowly ticked towards the witching hour, the time when the veils between the living and the dead were at their thinnest, a time and date where spirits were known to slip across the thresholds, something stirred in the darkness.

The thing was darkness itself. If it had been alive, then it would have fit in perfectly with the arrogance, with the sociopathic, uncaring maliciousness these nasty specimens exuded.

However, this thing wasn't alive.

It was perfectly un-alive.

The darkness of the room paled into insignificance against the obsidian nature of the thing that skulked within the walls. The overly long arms, with its spindly fingers stroked, and preened the sleeping boys. Where the shadowy digits touched them, they would squirm and wriggle, absently flick away the troublesome fly, or insect that was crawling over their susceptible flesh with an irritable moan.

It brought cold with it. It was more than a breeze, but it wasn't quite a wind, yet it had all the callous, uncaring danger of a grave, of a hole dug deep into the freezing earth.

The long fingers played with the boys. It touched them, caressed them as if they were lovers, or even a caring parent. Yet lovers, true lovers, wouldn't elicit such revulsion.

It hissed as it crept. It was difficult to tell if the sound was real. It sounded gleeful, yet it could have easily been filled with malintent. Perhaps it was both.

It moved with an otherworldly grace that spoke of smoke in a wind, or sheets hanging blowing in a breeze. If any of the boys had woken, they might have dismissed the black-on-black silhouette as a drunken illusion, however they would not have dismissed the dangerous cold that elicited with it, as it cavorted between them.

It was here for a reason. It had been called.

The spirit was timeless, it was privy to the past sins of these boy's families, to the current cruelties, and more importantly to the horrors of a future that wasn't quite written yet. It was a culmination of many things, and it knew it shouldn't exist.

Yet exist it did. It was here to address its very existence, and to enjoy what it was about to do.

It had ten in its grasp, and it pondered, with devilish glee, on which to take first.

2

That Christmas Eve morning had started much as any other during the holidays. The boys, all of them in tune with each other's rituals from slumbering in the same chambers for the last few years, awoke at the same time; roughly around ten in the morning. They roused in their lavish beds to the smell of searing bacon wafting up from the kitchens. They knew the cooked meat would be accompanied by eggs, and freshly baked bread.

As it was Christmas Eve, the food would be accompanied by mead. A strong brew, to put a lining on their still full bellies from last night's celebrations.

Each boy yawned and stretched as they alighted their beds. Still wiping sleep from their wary eyes, they ignored the knock on the door that interrupted their morning rituals.

The knock came again.

Once more, it was ignored.

It was a game. The boys looked at each other, the smirks on their faces unbidden as they made the servants wait, laden with their heavy dishes of food and wine.

'Come in,' Tarquin eventually shouted, after the hilarity of their jape had passed, and the hunger for the food they were bringing became too much.

The door was opened, and three young ladies walked in, all carrying large plates filled with food. Bacon, eggs, sausages, cobs of fresh bread with lashings of salted, churned butter. Another girl entered struggling to carry two large jugs that were filled with a dark liquid.

'About time too,' Tarquin sniped at them. 'We're fucking starving in here. While you sluts were laughing and giggling in the kitchens, we've been made to suffer.' He emphasised his, not so playful, remarks by pinching one of the girl's behinds. It wasn't a playful pinch; Tarquin wasn't the playful kind. It was a cruel, and harsh assault that would no doubt leave a nice bruise for Christmas Day.

She squealed, much to the delight of Tarquin, and dropped the plate she was carrying. Some of the meat fell onto the floor.

Alistair stood, just in time to dodge a hot, falling sausage. 'You fucking cretin,' he admonished the poor girl. 'You almost burnt me then,' he cursed.

'I'm so sorry, sir,' she mumbled in an apology.

'You what?' Alistair hissed.

'I said I'm sorry,' sir she reiterated.

'Sorry doesn't cut it, you whore!' he snapped. 'We are now…' he counted the sausages on the floor. 'One, two, three… four sausages down. How are we supposed to function on a lesser breakfast?'

'Would you like me to pick them up for you, sir?' the girl asked. Alistair could see the terror in her eyes, and this spurred him on.

'Pick them up?' he roared.

The rest of the boys were watching this with rapture. The other serving girls were wincing, knowing what was about to happen.

'Pick them up? Do I look like a fucking pauper to you? Do I look like your shit-stinking father?'

The girl shook her head.

'What? I never quite heard that. I asked, do I look like your shit-stinking father?'

'No, sir. You don't,' the cowed girl whispered her reply.

'You will address me as Lord Alistair, at all times. Do you hear me, you slut? Now I want to hear you tell me that I don't look like your shit-stinking father.'

She looked at the other girls, tears were welling in her eyes.

'Tell me,' Alistair roared. A rising giggle emitted from the other boys who were now tucking into their breakfasts.

'You don't look like my shit-stinking father, Lord Alistair.'

He looked at the girl, and a smile spread across his face. 'You lot,' he said, pointing towards the other serving girls who had plated the breakfasts, and poured the wine. 'You are all dismissed. Everyone, except this one.'

The girls, with their heads bowed, all left the room, leaving the unfortunate girl in the centre of the boys, her head bowed, sobbing.

'Do you know who we are, whore?' he spat.

She nodded.

'Then you will know of the Bullingdon Club. And you'll know that we get what we want when we want it. So now, I want you to undress. I want to see the bruise on your arse that Tarquin so graciously gave to you. Do it, now.'

The boys stopped eating, and all began to chant. 'Take it off… take it off… take it off.'

The girl looked around, hoping for help, for some solidarity from some quarter. However, nothing was forthcoming. All her friends and colleagues had gone, and the ten boys who were left were all leering at her, grinning while they ogled her, chewing their meat, loudly.

'We're waiting,' a smaller boy spat, his twisted face filled with malice.

'Easy, Cameron,' Tarquin laughed. 'I know you've never seen a naked woman before, and that you're looking forward to sticking it to the pigs head tonight but calm down. Alistair might allow you a slice of this one.'

'After I've finished with her, obviously,' Alistair laughed, grabbing his crotch.

The girl was sobbing as she removed her clothing, to the cheers, and the jeers of the Bullingdon Boys.

'There you go. That didn't hurt, did it?' Alistair said as he slowly stood up and took the naked girl's hand. 'Now, as you were so quick to pick up those fallen sausages, come with me, and I'll show you another sausage you can pick up.'

This caused a raucous cheer from the boys.

'And after you've finished with mine, I will implore you to work on Cameron's. You see he is rather eager to pop his cherry, so to speak.'

The girl was in tears as she took Alistair's offered hand, and he pulled her, roughly towards one of the sleeping chambers. He grinned as the girl, with the red welt on her backside, followed him like a broken-in, domesticated animal.

The boys continued eating, while the sounds of the girl screaming, and crying in the next room, cut through their chatter, and laughter.

Very soon Alistair reappeared, fixing himself. He looked at Cameron and grinned. 'She's all yours,' he laughed. 'I've stretched her enough for you, my boy. I think you'll get a bit more enjoyment from this one, than the pig's head tonight.'

This caused more laughter, as the thin bespectacled boy made his way into the room.

~~~~

Less than five minutes later, a bruised and beaten serving girl ran from the common room. Her body was red, and she was struggling to cover her nakedness and stop the blood running from her noise, and trickling between her bruised thighs, at the same time.

3.

The town of Oxford hated these boys, almost as much as the serving staff in the university campus. They strode through town, always in a group, dressed in their finest clothing. Black dining suites, top hats, white gloves, black cloaks with red silk linings, and canes. They looked like a flock of exotic birds as they swooped towards the various drinking parlours and taverns.

As they passed through the market, they helped themselves to anything, and everything from the stalls. Anything that caught their fancy was theirs for the taking. Trinkets, pies, fruit, candles, anything whether they needed it or not. They would take it, and they would move on, unquestioned by the traders, undisputed by the market managers. No one would challenge them, as to do so would surely bring down the wrath of their fathers, and their families. This would mean larger, unaffordable rents on their houses, or even eviction. It would mean higher taxes on their incomes, more tariffs on their market stalls, a lot more trouble than it was worth.

Today, the snow was thick on the ground, and the temperatures in Oxford were plummeting. It was still cold enough to snow, but the clouds were thinning dangerously, threatening to refreeze the already frozen streets.

A man was sat on the floor, huddled next to the door of a shop, obviously attempting to gleam as much warmth from the opening as he could. His eyes lit up as he saw the ten youths approach. Their expensive cloaks and good quality winter boots made them good candidates for a little charity to come his way. He sat up a little straighter than he had been and picked up the small tin he had before him. He rattled it towards his, and his family's, approaching saviours.

The few low denomination coins inside made a racket as he shook it. It caught the attention of the youths, and one of them tapped a colleague on the shoulder, indicating him.

The wretch's heart began to beat faster. Maybe this would be the Christmas miracle he'd been praying for. Maybe now he might find him, his wife, and their two children, somewhere to sleep for the night, and wake up warm on Christmas morning.

'Spare a penny?' he asked as a tubby boy with unruly blond hair approached him.

The boy grinned.

The man could see benevolence in the boys cherub-like face.

'Let's see if we can do a little better than a penny, eh?' the boy replied with a smile. He reached into his cloak and pulled out a leather wallet.

The man eyed it with the look of a drowning man eyeing a rope. The blond boy pulled out a large note. He unfolded the paper and showed it to the man.

His eyes widened as he regarded it. It was a five pound note, enough for somewhere to stay for the whole of the Christmas season. It would mean proper meals for his children, maybe even some new clothes.

It meant survival through the coldest of Christmases.

'Would you like this?' the blond boy asked, the look in his eyes changing. It was less benevolent now, and a little more mocking.

The man licked his dry, dirty lips.

'Would you?' he asked again.

The man nodded.

'I thought so.'

He put the note in the man's tin.

The wretch's throat was too dry to thank him properly. 'Sir…' was all he managed.

The blond boy looked at him. His pig-like eyes were blazing now. Not with anger, but with malice. 'I am *not* your sir,' he snapped. 'I'm your *Lord!*' He then fished into his inside pocket and produced a flint. He scraped the contraption into the tin. The sparks caught on the dry paper of the currency. The poor man's face dropped in denial of what he was watching. His salvation, his family's very survival was burning away before him. The note caught the flames so fast; he could barely believe it.

The fat blond boy stood and turned towards his colleagues. They were all laughing.

'Here, let me help you put that out,' he said, turning back to the man. He undid the buttons on his fly and removed his flaccid penis. The beggar didn't know where to look, at the appendage the boy had just removed, or at his Christmas, burning away in his tin. A thin stream of yellow urine spilled from the boy. It splashed over the freezing beggar, and also doused the flames of the burning currency within the tin. The note was ruined. It was now no more than a charred scrap of sodden paper. The man watched his salvation wither under the boy's flow. He saw his family hungry, cold, destitute. He saw his wife selling herself to buy bread, he saw his youngest, Martha, dead in the churchyard, the cold having eaten into her soft flesh, taking her to the real Lord, far too soon.

He bared what was left of his teeth and jumped at the fat boy.

'Boris, look out,' someone shouted from the group. It was a tall youth, one with a sly, long face, not unlike a donkey's, but with real odium in his eyes.

Boris, who was laughing as he buttoned up his fly, turned just as the man was on him. The fear in Boris' face was complete, revealing his cowardice. He managed to dodge the feeble attack and run back into the safety of the other boys. However, the man hadn't finished his attack. He ploughed into the crowd, swinging his fists. He connected with a few of them, feeble, weakened punches rained down on the startled, but delighted youth. Boris was at the back, shouting for someone to control the raging wretch.

The boys regrouped.

Cameron, fuelled by the fact that he had not long lost his virginity, and also beaten the serving wench almost to a pulp, pushed the man. It was not a hard push, but it was enough to knock the malnourished beggar to the floor. The man wailed, a pathetic moan, as he hit the snow-lined pavement. The cry rallied the ten young lords, especially Boris, who had been cowering at the back, like a pack of cowardly scavengers, sensing a weakened prey.

They all began to kick him. They were not merely playful kicks; these were full body blows. With their good quality snow boots, they did the wretch some serious damage.

There were many witnesses to this attack, however, after a couple of threatening glares, these witnesses blended into the cold, misty backdrop of the Oxford Christmas Eve. This wasn't because of a fear of a beating, these boys were nothing but cowards when on their own, but because the people knew their reputations, and more importantly their family's reputations, and connections. Interfering with these situation would cost them more trouble than the good people of Oxford needed.

The poor man was covering his face while crying in pain, and shame. Yet the blows continued. They only stopped when the mewling of the pathetic, unfortunate stopped, and the blood from his face, and from other parts of his body, began to flow.

Boris sneered. He pulled his leg back and delivered one last, vicious blow. There was a sickening *crack,* and all the boys laughed as they walked away, as one, leaving the beggar shaking, and dying, nursing broken ribs, and other sever injuries, in the freezing snow.

4.

The venture into the town, for the Bullingdon Boys was not just a frivolous chore. They were there to procure something special for their Christmas celebrations. There were two new members to initiate into the club tonight, and there were traditions they had to adhere to.

However, prior to doing what they came to do, there was fun to be had, paupers and oiks for them to play with and torment.

On entering a local tavern, they ordered drinks all around, three per man. The round was not paid for, instead it was put it on their *tab,* a tab that was already stretching the landlord to near breaking point. This was the last thing he needed on Christmas Eve as he still had to pay for the delivery of ale, he would need for the town's festivities tonight.

As the boys drank, they abused his customers, to a degree that most of them left the establishment, to continue their festivities unmolested elsewhere. Women where inappropriately approached, manhandled, and roughhoused, some were slapped and groped. When the men approached the boys, they were threatened, not with violence, but with their other weapons, financial threats. The men would back down as they knew these boys were not only *able* to back up these threats, they were *likely* to do it too.

The Bullingdon Boys would laugh, they would shout, and they would smash up whatever they pleased, tankards, chairs windows, anything, with total disregard for anyone other than themselves.

As they left, leaving a trail of destruction and a large unpaid bill, in their wake, the landlord sighed a deep sigh of relief. As he picked up the broken chairs, and the overturned tables, and mopped up the spilt, unpaid for ale, he thanked the good Lord they'd gone.

Their reign of terror continued on through the town. Shops were looted, property was damaged, and people were assaulted on the streets, as these ten, privileged, young *gentlemen* continued to use the town as their personal playgrounds.

Eventually, they got to where they were meant to be. It was a small butcher shop on the outskirts of town. They had put their order in prior to the Christmas period, and they knew the butcher wouldn't let them down on their order.

It was in his best interests not to.

They had procured a local farmer's prize swine, much to his chagrin as it was a fine stud. However, the farmer had learned the hard way not to disappoint the Bullingdon Boys club.

The pig had been procured, and paid for, a lot less than he would have demanded on the open market, or even if he had continued putting the fine beast out for stud. It had been delivered to the butcher, and the slaughter of the animal had occurred.

'You man,' the tallest of the boys, the one with the long, gormless face, shouted as he adjusted his spectacles. 'Do you have our order, you oik?'

The rest of the boys laughed at this put down. It happened to be one of their favourites. The pig's head was procured, put into a sack, and the boys, made their way back to the campus, much to the relief of the town.

~~~~

And so, they all came together, in the plush, warm common room, as the bells of the various churches of Oxford rang out their tolls to welcome in the Saviour's Day. They were all asleep, and the severed pig's head had been well and truly violated in the time-honoured way the elite had thought a good idea, for hundreds of years.

The boys were all asleep.

Safe and warm in their common room, drunk, satiated in their debauchery, content to wallow in the filth of their behaviour.

As they slept, various things happened within the town.

The poor serving girl, who had been violated by the two boys, took a broken bottle to her wrists. She cut deep, and she cut vertical, relishing the pain, and the heavy flow of blood that came with it. As her life ebbed away from, she cursed the boys she worked for.

She cursed them to Hell.

The wretch in the street had crawled into a corner, in the shelter of the churchyard where he had left his family to go begging in the street. The beating he'd taken had broken something inside him. The pain, the agony was too much for his emancipated body to heal. As he died, shivering, coughing up warm blood, his last thoughts were of his family. They would be waiting for him, less than a hundred yards from where he was. These thoughts were preceded by the faces of the cowards who had done this to him.

He cursed their very lives.

All ten of them, he cursed them all to Hell.

The man's wife, having been informed of her husband's beating, had gathered her two children to her breast. As they attempted to shelter from the snowstorm that was blanketing the town with its beautiful white covering of certain death, she, and her children froze to death. Before she passed, she cursed the boys of the Bullingdon Club, she cursed them all to Hell.

The tavern owner, with his profits way down due to the violence of the boys, and their stubborn refusal to pay their bill missed the payment of his ale, and would have to close for the night, destroying any hope of making enough for the month's rent, cursed the boys to Hell.

The farmer, whose livelihood for the next year would now be severely depleted due to the slaughter of his prize animal, for their nefarious enjoyment, cursed the boys to Hell.

Everyone they'd had dealings with over the year. Beatings, theft, underhanded deals, unwanted sexual advances… Everyone who knew these *boys*, cursed them, their families, and their future descendants, all to Hell.

~~~~

Something heard these curses.

Something took heed of what the people of Oxford were asking.

Something caught the unhappy spirits of the serving girl, the beggar, and his family. It derived strength from their dying curses and was given a mission.

And here it was, fulfilling that mission.

The darkness crept through the common room. It was desensitized to the debauchery around it. It didn't care for the boy's money, or their family connections. It was here for unbridled justice, and justice it would have.

The sleeping boys would be wakened.

The boys had been cursed to Hell, and it was here to deliver on that curse, to deliver the Hell promised. The first step on their journey was to know how they got to where they were, and for them to understand the helplessness of the situation. Their money, or their fathers were powerless to prevent what was to come.

It was now a predetermined course of action.

Nothing could stop it.

With a clap of its shadowy hands, the long, claw-like fingers caused a dark wave to flow through the room, awakening the boys.

Confusion reigned as they woke. They had fallen asleep drunk, and had expected to wake hung over, that was why they had ordered extra ale to be delivered, so they could continue the party, unheeded by hangovers. They were far too privileged, even for that indignity.

So, to find themselves sober, and wide awake as the bells pealed through the town, confused them.

'What is the meaning of this?' Tarquin asked sleepily, as he rubbed his eyes.

All of them saw the hideousness that had come to claim them, at the same time.

It was not a creature; it was not a being of any kind they could have identified, or even battled with, had that been in their nature. This was nothing more than darkness, within darkness. It was shapeless, yet there was form to it. It was swirling obsidian, unfocused and terrifying.

It had eyes. They were a lighter dark, almost purple. There was a density to them that unnerved the boys. The eyes morphed and stretched. Faces leered from the dark recesses of the bottomless holes. Faces of people the boys failed to recognised, but who recognised them. They were people, ordinary folk, crushed beneath the heels of these marauding pigs.

They were screaming, yelling, raging silently within the confines of the thing's eyes. The ten friends were entranced by them. None of them could remove their gazes from the faces they had harmed, from the individuals, families, communities they had ruined, decimated, destroyed with their callousness, and their self-serving greed.

The shadow shifted in the darkness.

No sound was made, yet it commanded them to move; and move they did, seemingly of their own volition. The ten youths walked to the large window, the one that opened over the freezing, cobbled courtyard, forty feet below.

The window opened. No one unlatched it, and no wind took it, it simply opened. A freezing wind whipped through it then, ruffling the young men's hair, causing their pyjamas to cling to them as they continued their slow march towards the wide-open window. When they reached their destination, they looked out, down the freefall to the dangerous, iced cobbles below.

The courtyard below was not empty, as each of them would have expected. In fact, it was far from it.

The space was filled to capacity. The spirits of the people these youths, their fathers, and their grandfathers, had all ruined, looked up at them. There were hundreds, maybe thousands of them all vying to watch justice delivered. Farmers, builders, merchants, men, women, children, even babies, stared up at the ten youths, their eyes and mouths hanging open, hungry to see just deserts.

One thought went through the minds of the young men looking down on the angry spirits.

Jump!

'*Do the world a favour,*' the dark spirit hissed. None of the youths turned to see who had spoken, it was taken that they knew. It was the voice of the great unwashed. The sobs, and cries of generations past, and generations their ilk will ruin, crush, and destroy in the years to come.

'*Your kind are nothing but filth. You are a smirch on the human race. Life should be about love, and sharing, and community, yet you seek only to enhance yourselves. You have no feeling for your fellow man. Our journey to the grave should be a happy one, filled with memories, and joy, yet you use your privilege to make it as difficult for everyone else you can. Do you think you are better than those down there? Well, why not let them know when you in their midst...*'

Each boy was shaking. Every one of them had wet their pyjamas. Their faces were pained with sorrow, with fear, with an understanding that they had brought this upon themselves. They cried and sobbed, beseeching with the spirt, telling them they would change, they had seen the errors of their ways.

They *would* be better men.

Their pleas fell upon deaf ears if the thing before even had ears.

A sense of a smile radiated from the thing, as it pointed to the window.

One by one, the ten Lords leaped, openly weeping, from the open window.

The fall took an eternity. Each boy reliving the Hell of their lives. Each feeling the pain and the suffering of the millions of people their kind would torment, and cheat to their graves, in the years to come.

As each boy crashed onto the hard, frozen cobbles, their skulls, ribs, backs, and necks shattered on the unforgiven stones beneath them.

However, that was not the end, or even the worst of it.

As their bodies broke, and their lives ebbed; their blood running along the channels between the worn cobbles, the gathered spirits descended upon them. Each wraith as eager as the next to get vent their ghostly anger on the Bullingdon Boys.

5

Christmas morning arrived with the customary peel of the bells. Families gathered to offer each other seasonal greetings. Churches opened their doors to welcome congregations, eager to receive a blessing from the new-born saviour.

However, all was not joyous, and gay. There were duties to perform, some not as enjoyable as others. Police had been called to various locations, to perform the sad task of removing the poor, unfortunate dead from graveyards, or from chambers, where serving girls slept.

The ten lords were found early in the morning by a gamekeeper, who was heading out for an early morning shoot. At first, he was shocked as his gaze fell on the twisted, broken bodies, then he was momentarily revulsed, and then he felt... elation.

He knew these boys, the ones with rictuses of pain, agony, and fear etched onto their frozen, blue faces. He knew their deaths would not elicit tears from anyone in the university, the town, or from anyone in the country, if he was honest.

The world was simply a better place without their kind.

He whistled a jaunty Christmas carol as he strode away, off to inform the police of the... what would he call it?

Oh yes.

A tragedy.

Eleven Pipers Piping
James Lefebure

The sickening music filled the room.

It had been five years since it had last enclosed the city. It hadn't left Sean's mind for a second since it first travelled into his brain. This cursed tune had changed his life. Glancing at the clock, he wasn't surprised to see it was one-minute past midnight. Across the city, he knew parents would be holding their children. They had all learned from the last time. Sean scanned the dusty bedroom. If he lost his sight this second, he could still navigate his son's brightly coloured bedroom. It was the centre of his world now. The rest of the flat was a cesspit of rubbish and broken dreams. This was the only space in what used to be his home that he had kept clean. Just in case.

Five years of searching for a surrogate. Four sessions of IVF. Three miscarriages. Two men determined to be fathers. One beautiful child. Those used to be the numbers of Sean's life. Five years of agony. Four years of marriage counselling. Three members of a family were destroyed. Two men who couldn't stand to be near each other. One missing child. These were the numbers of his life. *"You shouldn't have thought of Paul."* His mind hissed. The mere mention of his name, even in his mind, made his blood boil.

Joe's kidnap ruined their marriage. They had been so strong together during the surrogacy and the pregnancy. Sean knew that they were good parents. When you fight that hard to bring a soul into the world, you move heaven and earth to make sure they know they're loved. Sean was certain of one thing – Joe knew that his dads loved him. Then the music came. Its poisonous notes destroyed everything he and his family held close.

After that night, Sean was a man possessed. He hunted the streets, shadow filled bars, forbidden clubs and the dark side of Liverpool. This was a side of the city he called home, that he didn't know existed. The first year, his fists flew as fast as the blood he demanded in his search. Broken bones and bloodied faces amounted to very little. There was a belief that he had beaten out of an antique book dealer in Lime Street that said the Pipers would return. It was foretold. Just not when.

Paul did not react well to Sean's trip to the dark underbelly of his city. Paul did not want to fight. He wanted to cry. He lost a part of himself the night Joe "went missing." A phrase he used, which always boiled Sean's piss. Their son didn't "go missing." He was taken. Under the cover of pipe music and a magic that had no place in their world. Paul's spirit died that night. Along with Sean's respect for him. He couldn't be married to a man who had no fight. Turns out Paul couldn't be married to a man who wanted to fight either. One year later, almost to the day, Paul moved out.

The music got sharper. Sean could feel it hooking into his brain. His thoughts became thick as treacle. Images of pain and violence flooded his mind. Just like last time. The tune was the same as the last time. Sean however, had spent a lot of time reading up on The Pipers. With the last of his savings, he'd purchased a necklace from a jeweller off Mathews Street. The jewellery was a simple chain with a golden coin hanging in the middle. Sean knew the runes and etchings on the small coin like the back of his hand. He'd studied them for hours online to verify that the protection spell was legitimate. Sean stood and walked to the bedroom door. After three steps he knew the necklace was working. The last time he was frozen in place. Forced to watch as those things took his son.

Quiet as the rage burning in him, Sean crept down the corridor. He could hear movement in the front room. They were back. Peeking through the crack in the door, he saw two shapes moving around in the living room. The music stopped. The shapes were vaguely human – two legs, two arms but a hunched-over back and unseen head confirmed that they weren't. They were communicating in grunts that Sean couldn't understand. He didn't need to. Years of pain and despair travelled to his tightened fist. There was a moment, as he burst screaming into the room, that he knew this was a terrible idea. However, as his fist connected with the scaly flesh of the first creature, the thought disappeared. Piper One fell to the floor quickly as Sean pulverised its hideous face. It made crying noises until it started to choke on its sharp teeth that Sean punched into its mouth. Once it went limp, Sean spun on his heel and turned to face Piper Two. It stood frozen on the spot.

"Not expecting that was you, soft lad?" Sean's thick Liverpool accent spat across the room. Before it could answer, Sean flew across the room. His rough hands wrapped around the neck of the creature. As he crushed the throat of thing before him, he smiled for the first time in years. *"If only Paul could see this."* His mind congratulated as the creature started to slump.

"He had his chance." Sean shouted. Spittle flew from his lips and his grip tightened. When Piper Two sagged to the ground, he released his hands and let it fall.

"Fuck. You. Paul." He screamed at the memories that haunted the house. "I fucking told you!" Sean pointed at the two bodies on the floor. "I TOLD you I'd get them!" He could feel the tears on his face. "I told you." He half sobbed. Running his hand over his shaved head, Sean bent over and picked up the flute it had dropped.

The instrument was old. Very old. It felt wrong in Sean's hands. Dirty and full of malice. The urge to put it to his lips was as intense as the hatred he felt for the thing that he had taken it from. He put it in his back pocket. The hunt had begun. The reading he had done about these things, had hinted that there were eleven in total. That was the number. It was in the few sparse texts he could find. He had taken care of two. Kicking the body at his feet a final time, Sean turned and left the house. His feet carried him with an intention he didn't believe was his own. Outside he cast a glance at the house. Its days as home were no more. Now it would serve as a graveyard for the life he nearly had.

Walking down Park Road, Sean heard it. The soft notes of another Piper.

"Got ya" he whispered.

Not thinking about where he was going, Sean allowed his feet to carry him to his destination. Abruptly he stopped outside a house on Windsor Street. A reindeer and Santa flashed on and off outside the home. Through the blinds, he could see the twinkling of lights on a Christmas tree. The music had stopped but he knew in his gut there was a Piper in the house. Then he heard the screaming.

Jumping the gate, he ran to the open front door and rushed in. The aroma of cinnamon and pine greeted him first. Then he saw the blood. It was everywhere. Gagging, Sean saw the body of a man. Correcting himself, he saw the lower half of a body. The upper half was behind him, next to a pile of Christmas presents. The poor man's face had been clawed beyond recognition. The door to the kitchen opened. Piper Three walked into the room. It was almost double the size of the two that he had found in his house. Its black eyes locked onto Sean as it moved toward him.

"Boy is not here." It laughed. "Daddy in the wrong house." Its voice sounded so human, that for a second Sean forgot that this *thing* was not a man.

"The fuck did you say?" Sean asked. It knew who he was. What he was looking for.

"Boy does not want daddy now." It sounded bored as it lifted a bloodied arm to its mouth. Sharp teeth tore a chunk of meat and started to chew. "Boy wants the music." It announced with a mouth full of blood and flesh. Sean felt his stomach churn.

"Where is my son?" Sean screamed.

"Doesn't want daddy anymore." The creature laughed once more. "I will have daddy."

The laughter stopped suddenly as the creature, with a speed Sean never expected flew across the room and punched him in the stomach. Gasping for air, he tried his best to stand up. The creature was faster. He felt himself get picked up and crash into the Christmas tree. Baubles smashed as the tree toppled over with him in it. Piper Three took a single stride across the living room and grabbed Sean by the shirt.

"Daddy tasty?" It asked quizzically before pulling Sean towards him and biting his shoulder. Sean screamed as his flesh was ripped from his body. Thrashing with all his might, he couldn't escape. The creature's eyes never left Sean as it chewed the meat. Panic was setting in. Being eaten by one of these creatures was not how he planned the night going. Sean reached behind him as the creature pulled him closer for another bite. As the flute broke the flesh on the side of the creature's neck it dropped him. Sean had been in enough street fights to know not to waste the moment. The creature bellowed as it pulled the bloody flute from his neck and flung it across the room in disgust. Not missing a second Sean grabbed the closest weapon he could find – the metal star on top of the fallen Christmas tree.

The creature shrieked as Sean drove it through its eye. Viscous fluid burst over Sean's hand as he pushed the star in further. The creature fell backwards with a thud. Sean didn't waste time and continued the assault. The star became an extension of his arm as he stabbed repeatedly. Blood washed over him.

"Like that do you?" *Stab.* "Fucking." *Stab.* "Kid stealing." *Stab and twist.* "Cunt."

The mess that lay before him was dead. As was everyone else in the house. The silence, punctured by the gentle buzzing of the Christmas lights flashing, was all encompassing. His shoulder throbbed. He knew that it would need to be looked at, but not tonight. Not when there were Pipers still to be found.

"You need to look after yourself." Paul's voice whispered. Over the years, whenever he needed to do something for himself it was always Paul's voice that told him. Paul had always been the more maternal of the two. Sean was the bad cop. Paul was the good cop.

"Fuck off Paul." He whispered to the empty house. He walked out the house and into the night air.

With shaking hands, he lit a cigarette. Scanning the street with tired eyes he noticed there were no twitching curtains. Nobody stood on their step. The noise from the house had been ignored. *"They're scared."* Paul whispered in his mind.

"Oh, will you get to fuck, Paul." He told the empty street. "This isn't about you." Flicking the cigarette away he walked away from another family he couldn't save. The music would find him. He would find them. Then he would save his son. Once he had Joe, Paul might come back. They could fix their family. Sean allowed himself the simple luxury of daydreaming about this as his feet and hands continued to do his wet work.

And continue they did.

The daydream ended with a grunt and a tug. Piper Nine's face came away from its skull with a wet ripping. He had been picturing Joe's wedding. The ripped skin in his hands was a stark crash back to reality. Looking at the monstrosity on the floor, Sean was confident it was dead. He was close to the end now. Nine dead Pipers. The journey to his son was nearly over. Piper Nine had been very vocal about where to find Joe. In its own distorted tongue, it had told him to follow the music to the docks.

Sean felt the music scratching his brain as soon as he arrived at the Albert Dock. The closed shops reflected the dull streetlamps back at him as he wandered round the square. He knew they wouldn't be here; it was too open. He couldn't shake the feeling that he was close. Some part of him just knew that he would find something here. Limping away from the tourist area his feet carried him. The music floated across the Mersey.

"No way." He whispered as he stood in the cold shadow of the arena. The front door had been ripped off and lay discarded in the foyer. Glass crunched over the music as Sean stepped inside.

There were no lights inside the building. Sean winced as he turned his head to listen. The wound on his shoulder was not his only wound this evening. Piper Five had clawed Sean's face. Piper Seven had nearly ripped his arm off. Piper Eight had taken a bite out of Sean's thigh as it lunged at him. He was a tapestry of pain. It might have slowed him down, but it had not stopped him. Nothing would stop him from finding Joe tonight. The stakes had been laid out before him and he had chosen to play. Death was the consolation prize for the game and Sean was not going to be a runner up tonight.

Despite living in the city his whole life, Sean had never stepped foot in the giant Arena. Paul had gotten them both tickets for some band they both liked for Christmas *that* year. They had never gotten used. He couldn't even remember the name of the band now. Sean walked deeper into the heart of the building. The smell of stale popcorn and beer was overpowering. His stomach grumbled in protest. Sean ignored it. His focus was on the music. It was getting louder.

Sean pulled open a double door to the arena. Despite his eyes trying to become accustomed to the dark, he tripped over something. The fall knocked what little wind was left in him. He lay there for a moment. The pain pulsed through his body. He took three deep breaths and used his good arm to push himself into a sitting position. The music surrounded him. This was the right part of the building. A movement to his right caught his attention. Ignoring the pain, Sean stood up. It took him longer than he would have wanted, but he was upright. He saw what he had tripped over.

"Help" a thin voice whispered. Sean rushed to the side of the security guard whose legs had caused him to greet the ground.

"Jesus, mate" Sean whispered as he knelt, ignoring the wave of nausea that washed over him. "What happened?" "Monsters." The weak voice replied. The man's right cheek was a bloody mess. Something had tried to rip a chunk off. "Tried. Eat. Me." The man coughed wetly. Sean felt blood coat his face.

"How many were there?" Sean asked, wiping absently at his face.

There was no reply.

"Mate." He shook the man. "How many are there?"

"My face." The man whimpered. Slowly, he lifted his hands to his face. "My face?" he asked again.

"It's fucked." Sean didn't see the point of lying. The man wouldn't be alive much longer. "How many were there?" he repeated.

"My face!" the man screamed as his hand touched the bloody mess that was once a cheek. His scream seemed to fill the entire area.

"Shut up!" Sean hissed. The man continued to scream and moan as he woke from the stupor he had been in.

"HELP! HELP ME!" He bellowed as his hands flew to Sean's top.

"Shut the fuck up mate." Sean whispered as he tried to pull the man's hands away from him. He didn't think he would have the element of surprise. However, this man was giving his exact location away. Then it dawned on him.

This was a trap.

"It hurts," the stranger wailed. "My face."

With a yank Sean pulled free from the bloodied panicked grip of the man. He needed to get away. The music had stopped. His bones clicked as he stood upright again.

"I'm sorry." He whispered as he walked away from the man. There was nothing he could do for him.

"Please. Don't leave me." The stranger wailed. His sobs danced around Sean as he walked into the darkness. There was no time for mercy. The trap had been sprung and Sean knew that with every passing minute his chances of leaving the arena shrunk. Sean resisted the urge to look behind him. The man's fate was sealed.

There was a stage set up for some concert that had escaped his notice. The music filled the arena. Sickly sweet notes danced around him. Piper Ten was stood on the stage. The flute glowed as the notes escaped. Their power now undeniable. Sean could feel the notes scratching inside his head. Memories of Paul and Joe flooded his mind. He gripped the necklace, hoping this would help boost its power. It was a futile gesture.

"Oi knobhead." Sean's voice had a bravado that his heart did not feel.

His body ached. The adrenaline that had been fuelling him was waning. He could feel every bite, cut, and scratch that this journey had gifted him. He wished Paul was here. Paul, with his sensible and sensitive ways, would have talked him out of this. Paul, the only one who could have stopped him, had left him to this. Tears fell freely down his face as the music continued. The Piper didn't stop his tune as Sean climbed up on the stage. His muscles screaming. His heart breaking. The song continued.

Legs shaking, Sean locked onto the Piper. The small frame was hidden under a dirty cloak. Thin hands held the flute to unseen lips. Sean licked the sweat off his lips. The world lurched for a second. His jelly legs barely held him as he took an uncertain step towards the creature.

"Don't ignore me." Sean threatened weakly. He could hear pain in his voice. It blended with the music. His head swam.

"Please." He whispered. His necklace was failing to protect him from the music. The thirst for blood and vengeance, while not stated, was waning. The horrors of the night danced to the notes in his mind. So much blood. Too much suffering. A flurry of innocence defiled in his quest. The music stopped.

"Daddy." The stranger sighed. "Music for Daddy."

Sean's stomach lurched. This wasn't the first Piper to taunt him with a dead title. However, this time it felt different. There was emotion. A connection. Something passed between them. Sean felt the pain of the word that passed his lips.

"Joe?"

"Music for Daddy." The piper repeated. His thin hand pulled the cloak off his head. The face it revealed was a patchwork of scars. Smooth and pale. Red angry welts stood out across its skull. Dry cracked lips mouthed something that Sean couldn't hear over the sound of his sob. Older and thinner. This creature was his son.

"What have they done to you?" He wailed as he limped across the stage. Tears burned his eyes. His heart was racing. Fangs flashed as the creature smiled.

"Music for Daddy?" It pushed his flute towards Sean, who ignored it and wrapped his arms around the ghost that used to be his son. There was no resistance. It didn't return the affection. Sean didn't care. He couldn't let go. He wouldn't let go. His sobs filled the silence as he wept for the years he'd lost. For the pain that had been dished out to his boy. The rage that had fuelled him reignited at the idea of someone hurting his boy. Kneeling before the impossible, Sean looked into the eyes of the creature. There was a spark of something left in there. He could see that something in Joe's eyes remembered him. Sean would remind him. He would take him away from this. He could begin to repair his family. He wouldn't be alone anymore.

"Daddy hurt friends." Joe's tone changed. Sean could hear the sadness of his accusation.

"They weren't your friends', baby." He whispered through his tears. "They took you from us."

Sean couldn't let go of Joe's thin hand. He ignored the claws that had replaced his nails. The dried blood around fingers. When he looked at his son's face, he didn't see the blood around his mouth. This was his family. "I'm sorry." He pacified. "I'm so, so sorry." In that moment he was. This night had been a quest and now he was claiming his prize. Revenge had been the goal. Not treasure.

"Daddy play." Joe pulled himself away from Sean's iron grip with a strength that he shouldn't have had for his frame. The space he left behind clawed at Sean's heart. He couldn't bear it.

"Play." Joe repeated in a growl. He passed the flute to Sean. "Join." Joe's voice had a giddy sing song quality.

"I can't." Sean sobbed as he took the flute. Its metallic coldness burned his hand. Nine dead Pipers hadn't prepared him for this. Nothing had prepared him for this. Hours of research. Months of reading on the myths of the pipers, there had been no mention of what had happened to those that were taken. Just the number. There needed to be eleven. Eleven Pipers. Sean had reduced their number. But he couldn't diminish it further. There would be no more bloodshed tonight.

"Play." Joe urged. "Join." Joe looked at his father. "Please Daddy." His voice sounded human long enough for Sean to put the instrument to his lips. It burned his flesh, but he didn't care.

"Join Daddy." The words from his son muted the pain. Sean played. He joined. Time slowed as sad notes of pain escaped from Sean's breath. His agony filled the stadium. Shattered dreams and plans danced around the empty space. Sean's skin peeled and changed. Memories of a family that no longer existed accompanied his pain. He couldn't differentiate between which hurt more. He breathed through the claws that ripped through his fingers as they moved of their own will up and down the flute. The notes were no longer unknown to him. Knowledge of a dark history flooded his changed brain.

Joe hopped from foot to foot, his happiness written over his broken face. Sean couldn't hear the words that he was saying over the music. His thoughts became muddied as the notes filled his head and changed his body. With a final sharp note the song was done.

"Daddy." Joe shrieked happily as his thin arms wrapped round the thing that used to be Sean. They were together again.

"Boy." Sean laughed in a stranger's voice returning the love. Sean could feel himself, the real self, fading. He was content. He had his son. His family was nearly complete. Two Pipers together. They would need more though. He knew this.

"Daddy Paul." Sean coughed. His mouth still felt alien to him.

Joe clapped excitedly. Sean smiled.

"Daddy Paul. Play. Join." The smile on Joe's face was the second last thing Sean would experience before he disappeared. The last was a simple thought.

"My family will be whole again."

Twelve Drummers Drumming
Stephen Cooper

Twas was the night before Christmas, and there were dicks everywhere.

Lady wasn't interested in traditional Christmas porn, she didn't give a fuck about sexy Santa's, or naughty little elves who needed to be punished with candy cane dildo's, she cared about cock, and a lot of it. A buffet of dick. She wanted twelve guys slapping their hard rods against her face, *Twelve Drummers Drumming* their meat against her cheeks on Christmas Eve.

And in return, they were promised a warm Christmas meal. Turkey, stuffing, gravy, all the trimmings, including pigs in blankets. The works.

Naturally all twelve homeless guys she'd invited to the shoot took her up on the offer.

A warm meal and getting to cum all over Lady's face, *it was a fucking Christmas miracle*. All she asked in return was they followed her instructions to the letter, or as she called it, her recipe.

Instinctively, a couple of them were dubious. Christmas miracle or not, hot thirty-year-olds with Lady's enormous tits didn't often ask for a giant orgy on Christmas Eve with a bunch of smelly homeless guys she didn't know from Adam. Some of them could have been dangerous, *several were*, but she reassured them her requests were nothing they wouldn't't agree to.

"Just some harmless Christmas fun," she'd winked to the group. "A little Christmas tradition."

Her apartment looked sufficiently christmasy for the shoot. Tacky decorations were pinned to the ceilings, a fake tree was chock full of dangling ornaments of reindeer and snowmen. A fairy stood atop the tree looking all sweet and innocent with her halo overhead, oblivious to the depravities which were about to take shape in front of her. Presents sat under the tree. Fake snow covered the windows, concealing the spacious apartment from the outside world so they could fuck in peace. The back wall was covered in a Christmas mural depicting the twelve days of Christmas.

The whole place smelt lovely as the waft of cooked meat floated in the air of the open planned kitchen. Cut vegetables sat on the side. Serving plates were stacked, ready to be filled.

As soon as the Twelve Drummers - as they'd been dubbed - all arrived, Lady stripped off. Their collective faces lit up like a kid on Christmas morning, except it was Christmas Eve and they weren't getting a brand-new games console, they were getting to fuck Lady.

Their younger selves would have been very happy with the trade.

She'd considered some of the 'sexy 'Christmas outfits, but they'd just get in the way. Naked was the way to go... *and it was the easiest way to gain their trust.* She ordered them to all strip too, "Christmas dinner is waiting," she informed, leaving it in no uncertain terms that she meant herself.

Lady took her place on a long table immaculately set up in the middle of the room. Christmas crackers sat next to each perfectly presented plate. Sizeable gaps were left along the table ready for the serving dishes, but what was currently being served up was Lady. She hopped onto the table, her bare-naked peach ass barely missing a fork beneath it and laid back spreading her legs for all twelve guys to get a good look at her glistening cunt.

"Merry Christmas boys."

She winked to the camera set up beside them, then beckoned the first guy forward.

They took it in turns stuffing her as Lady angled her long legs wide apart and up in the air, like a cooked turkey, which is exactly what she kept calling her moist pussy.

"Stuff my turkey," she repeatedly shouted… they all obliged.

Those not stuffing her 'turkey, 'hummed jingles, while they waited their turn. Everyone quickly got into the Christmas spirit.

The camera filming the shoot was set up as a static wide shot which offered an angle of Lady's juicy pussy, and the sweaty dicks penetrating it. It wasn't exactly a dynamic production. There were no film lights, just the illumination offered from the Christmas lights blinking through-out the apartment, and the regular everyday lights switched on overhead. A couple of the homeless guys offered to wield the camera, add a little flair to the shoot, but Lady declined, much to their confusion. She had a certain style of shooting and the position it stood would suffice. Her audience had a specific taste she informed.

✳

After they'd all had a few pumps, *'stuffing her like a turkey,* 'any doubts of Lady's motives dissipated. If she was playing them in some way, well, fuck it, they'd all gotten to get their dicks wet. It beat laying in a doorway in the freezing winter snow thinking how another Christmas was passing them by. Even if the warm Christmas dinner didn't come to fruition, it was better than the last couple of shitty Christmases. The dinner at the soup kitchen was ok, but they didn't get to fuck some hot blonde first. *Santa had come early.*

Bizarrely, Lady hadn't even asked them to wash their rancid cocks but did give the option beforehand. Half took her up on the offer and had a rare shower in her luxurious apartment. She'd even brought a Christmas scented shower gel to add to the festivities.

The other half who didn't wash fulfilled an often thought about fantasy as they got to *take* the sort of woman who often looked down on them in the streets, while still being covered in filth. Sticking it to the man, *or in this case, slutty woman.* Lady didn't seem to mind.

The second request was for gravy, as Lady put it. It basically meant cumming all over her face and tits. Again, there weren't any objections as she laid completely naked on the made-up Christmas table with her perfect cunt on display, her enormous perky tits defying gravity, and her hungry mouth opened wide.

While they weren't allowed to cum as they fucked her, *which somehow, they all managed to stick too,* this time not only was it desired, but impossible not too. A couple had only got a few pumps the first time round before they had to pull out, this time, loads were shot in record time.

Some was because of the absurdity of the situation, mixed with Lady's beauty, while others hadn't been with a woman in far too long. Pent up frustration that they finally got to release on Christmas Eve. Their present this year, and what a present it was as some jerked it over her, while others enjoyed Lady's delicate hands stroking their excited peckers. There was plenty of high-fives and howls.

None of the twelve had been concerned with appearing in a porno. Any such reservations had been stripped from them long ago. Lady had done her homework. None had any family they were in touch with. None of them had any kind of ironclad morals, *or dignity for that matter.* The street had beaten it from them. One freezing cold winter too many.

And the promise of pussy and a roast trumped any remaining worries.

No one was going to see them in this smut, so who gave a fuck. Might as well enjoy it. A few even smirk at the camera from time to time, but Lady always directed their faces away from the prying lens.

"It's your cock they want to see."

*

The next request took the dozen homeless guys by surprise. They knew there had to be a catch, and this definitely felt like it, but it wasn't what they'd expected. They all thought she'd maybe be in to a little pain, *causing or receiving judging by her behaviour,* or make them do some stuff to each other, which a couple of them were down for. But nope.

Lady wanted to shave their pubes?

They couldn't't quite get their head around it. *Why?*

A couple questioned the odd request, against their better judgment, but Lady didn't seem to mind the issue being raised despite her earlier demand that they follow her instructions to the letter.

"Trimmings," she told them, like it explained absolutely fucking everything. "To complete the meal," she offered, as further explanation to the bewildered dozen.

"Trimmings?" They asked back.

"You got to stuff my turkey and cover me in gravy, the last part of a Christmas meal is trimmings, and this is the best I could come up with for my audience." She pointed to the camera like it made perfect sense.

Who doesn't want to see a bunch of homeless dudes getting their pubes shaved for a Christmas porn video?

Collectively, they all knew she was out of her fucking mind, but what the hell. She'd been a good sport so far, and if she had some kind of weird shaving fetish, so be it.

And if that's what the audience wanted to see...

"You want me to trust you with a razor against my cock?" The most well-endowed of the bunch asked. He might not have had much in life, but he still had a big veiny dick, and he wasn't eager to risk his prized possession.

"If you want my Christmas pudding," Lady countered, turning her gorgeous naked body to the group, and spreading her cheeks to give them all a good look at her puckered delicious asshole.

Hands shot up for who would go first as the Christmas presents continued to flow. Whatever kind of bizarre shoot this was, everyone was all in, even the cautious big dick relaxed.

The power of a good ass.

Lady spent the next hour carefully trimming their pubes. She guided the razor with expert precision like she'd done this a thousand times, no hair left untouched. The guys took it in turns like they were at the fucking barbers, each enjoying the touch of Ladies skilled hand. She even gave them a quick suck once the shave was complete… as a reward. *Beats a lollipop at the dentist.*

When all the cocks were cleanly shaved Lady promised them, desert was right around the corner, grabbing her ass an extra emphasis, but she needed one more thing first.

Lady provocatively led the manscaped dozen to the back room in her apartment, making extra sure to shake her shapely ass with each and every step. They were all practically drooling, despite already getting to have plenty of dirty fun with the sexy sultress.

The room looked like some kind of BDSM room, but she wasn't interested in any of the toys on display, or the chains and whips they had all secretly feared earlier might be her kink. *Although a couple of them would be into it.*

Instead, she got them to line up against a plastered board wall which led back to the living room.

The glory hole wall, as she dubbed it.

Twelve spaces, for twelve freshly shaved cocks.

Each glory hole was decorated like the twelve days of Christmas from the other side. None had spotted the holes in the Christmas mural as they'd approached the room as all of them were too busy marveling at Lady's ass, anticipating ramming their cocks up it. *The only hole left untouched.*

Lady moved the camera in position as the men took their places the other side, none quite sure what was going on. She threw on a best of Christmas playlist as each guy stuck his freshly shaven cock through the holes letting their dicks hang against the mural to the sound of Christmas tunes. It was quite the site. A couple of them couldn't't help but laugh. Weird fucking night, but the best Christmas they'd all had in a long time.

"Twelve Drummers Drumming," Lady joked to the group, seeing all the meat slapping against the wall. She began to move down the line briefly sucking each of their dicks until every one of them was hard as granite once again. She stopped at the end of the wall as the last cock left her mouth with a pop.

"I forgot part of the meal," she told them.

"What?" They collectively asked, wondering what crazy shit they'd get to do to her this time.

"Pig's in blankets," she revealed, with a sudden change in tone. It was a lot more sinister than the flirty voice she'd been using through-out the evening. A lot more… dangerous.

None of the Twelve had time to react to the disconcerting change.

*

Lady pulled a lever disguised as a candy cane drum stick on the Christmas mural.

Razor sharp steel wire slashed down from above every hole the hard cocks stood from. The wire easily sliced through the dozen dicks severing them instantly and sending the loose meat to the floor below as blood sprayed from the wall like some kind of macabre Christmas water feature.

Anguished howls echoed from the room behind the wall. One moment the merry men were getting their dicks sucked and singing Christmas carols, the next their cocks were all over the fucking floor!

The twelve men dropped in unison as blood continued to spray from the newly created holes where their dicks once proudly stood. The crimson jetted all over the room as the twelve drummers squirmed in unbearable pain and tried to make sense of what the fuck had happened. Shock had well and truly taken control.

What the fuck?

They just wanted their dicks sucked, now they didn't even fucking have one.

How was that possible? Fuck!

Lady let the nearest of the twelve stumble through the door before she locked it, trapping the remaining eleven inside. There was nowhere to go within the room, and the blood was coming thick and fast. The plasterboard wall may not have been the thickest, but they were in no shape for some great escape. And if they did try, she'd fucking stab them with the carving knife sitting on the kitchen side. *All part of the Christmas fun.*

The twelfth man fell to the floor screaming about his lack of dick, still uncertain what happened. He'd felt a sharp pain, like maybe Lady had bitten him, *and even liked it a little at first,* but then something felt wrong. Very fucking wrong. More so when he discovered his dick was no longer attached to his fucking body. His pride and joy was gone. The only thing he had in this shitty fucking world was no more. *And for what?*

His balls had got caught in the cross fire too and laid a split mess next to his cock.

Why'd he shove the whole package through?

He pleaded for help as he laid dying on the ground, but Lady had no intention of helping. In fact, she was still one ingredient short, so things were potentially going to still get a lot worse for the poor fellow. Mercifully though, Lady stabbed him in the throat, putting him out of his misery before she began to carve strips of skin from his recently cleaned body. She was tempted to use the potato peeler for more even strips, but last year it had jammed pretty fucking quickly. 'If in doubt, use a knife, 'her mother always instructed, and Lady always done what her mother told her.

Afterwards, Lady turned the camera off, and gathered the cocks from the floor. She took them in to the kitchen as she hummed along to the Christmas tunes blasting in the background thinking how enjoyable the Christmas Day movie would be this year.

Was definitely going to be better than her sisters three wise men snuff flick from last year.

The last of the dying groans faded from the room behind her as Lady began to wrap the liberated cocks in the fleshly diced skin, creating her own special version of Pigs in Blankets. It was a favourite, and something Lady always brought round her parents for the family Christmas dinner. There would be six of them around the table in total, so she cooked two each.

Her twelve drummers were no longer drumming, instead their cocks were cooking in the oven, as you can't have a nice Christmas dinner without pigs in blankets.

About The Authors

Mark MJ Green

Bald, bearded and bumbling, Mark likes the spooky side of life and things that go bump in the night. Although that's usually him wandering into something as he didn't bother to turn a light on.

Take one, Mr Potatohead. Attach his angry eyes - preferably placing one of them at a slightly different angle to the other. Affix a beard and leave the head barren of growth.

Congratulations. You now have your very own Mark Green.

Caution: Product may swear at random moments and for no apparent reason.

https://www.goodreads.com/.../show/20176631.Mark_M_J_Green

Renn White

Renn White is a horror fanatic and writer from Northumberland. She spends most of her free time roaming the woods, collecting inspiration for her horror stories. Renn's love of taxidermy and all things macabre shines through in her writing. As a self-described "horror fanatic," Renn draws from a wide range of influences, from classic horror literature to B-rated horror movies. Her writing aims to elicit both fear and wonder in her readers, tapping into the darkness that lurks within all of us.

Megan Stockton

Megan Stockton is an indie author who lives in rural Tennessee with her husband and two children. She has had a love for all things horror and macabre since she was a child and has been writing for fun most of her life. She enjoys delivering her readers horror and horror-adjacent works that are character-driven and immersive. You can find her complete list of works and social media links at meganstocktonbooks.com.

Angel Van Atta

Angel Van Atta was born to an abusive father and a mother who would soon fall victim to cancer's ugly fist. After the death of her mother, when Angel was just four years old, she was separated from her half-brother who had shared the same mom and bounced around from family members to friends of her father. Because of her curious and sometimes terrifying childhood, Angel soon turned to horror as a way to feel safe. She found that horror on the page or on the screen was often worse than what she was going through in real life, and in these stories there was hope as well as redemption and the coming together of the oppressed and terrified. But, most importantly, she found that good could triumph over evil. These were great comforts to the scared and lonely little girl. Angel is now a mother of two who was lucky enough to find a husband who was everything her father was not. Kind and trustworthy and good. She writes horror as a way to spread the same kind of hope that she so needed as a little girl and outside of the world of fiction only really ever found as an adult. Her stories are vivid and chilling as well as heartwarming and fast paced. She invites you to walk with her in her imagination. A place that can be just as dark as it is light.

Kelvin V.A Allison

Born in Portsmouth, England in 1973, Kelvin V.A Allison has somehow found his way to the hill strewn paradise that is County Durham, where he lives a life of calm and insanity in equal measure in the village home that he shares with his fiancée, and their four children.

An author of over forty novels, including the ten book World of Sorrow series, he is also an avid board gamer, and a lifetime fan of fruit filled sugared pastries. He would prefer it if you did not judge him.

D.W. Hitz

D.W. Hitz lives in Montana, where the inspiring scenery functions as a background character in his work. He is a lover of stories in all mediums and writes Extreme Horror, Horror, and supernatural/Paranormal.

Learn more about D.W. Hitz at www.DWHitz.com.

Lisa Hutchinson

Lisa Hutchinson is a born and bred native of the rolling hills and endless countryside of County Durham, England, where she enjoys the quiet life with her partner and two sons.

With a love of horror, and all things morbid and spooky, she began co-writing horror novels in 2020 with her bearded and wonderful friend Kelvin VA Allison. Lisa has now begun writing solo pieces, with Seven Swans being her first to be released.

Eric Butler

Eric Butler is an indie Horror writer who lives deep in the heart of Texas. When he's not writing novels and stories for anthologies, he's doing the bidding of 2 adorable huskies. He's been married for over 20 years and has a 21-year-old, so he won't be running out of horror material for quite some time.

https://linktr.ee/EricButlerAuthor

Lee Richmond

Lee Richmond was born in the swampy marshlands of East Anglia. Fed on a steady diet of fast, snotty punk rock and 80s slasher movies, it was only a matter of time before the sick, twisted imagery that festered in his head eventually found its way to the page.

Lee was influenced from a very early age by the films of John Carpenter, Dario Argento, Wes Craven, Sam Raimi and Tobe Hooper and the books of Clive Barker, Stephen King and James Herbert.

Music also plays its part in influencing Lee's writing. His love for bands like The Misfits, Ramones, Fugazi, Operation Ivy, Black Flag, Bad Religion, and Sisters of Mercy and the works of such movie composers as Hans Zimmer and Christopher Young.

Lee's other interests include playing bass guitar and drawing. He also hosts the reelhorrorshow podcast along with fellow writer, Mark MJ Green. Lee is a freelance writer and editor for hire. As well as writing books, he has recently been picked to write the screenplay for an up-and-coming Friday the 13th fan project. If you wish to know more, then please feel free to contact Lee on one of his social media pages or at Goodreads.

DE McCluskey

DE MCCLUSKEY - lives for Christmas all the year round... he single handedly keeps the Hallmark Film channel in business... this overwhelming influx of cheesy Christmas fluff warps his mind for the rest of the year, enabling him to write some twisted stuff. Check him out at www.the-erotic-elf.cum or Dammaged.com

James Lefebure

Aberdeen Born, Liverpool Living author who has been a fan of the horror genre since his first Goosebumps book back in the 80s.
Can often be found trading at comic cons, horror cons, and comic markets. Or reading horror and forcing his long-suffering partner to watch Candyman because "it's a romance movie really!"

Firm believer that Jason would absolutely beat Michael in a fight!

Stephen Cooper

Stephen Cooper is an Extreme Horror Author from Portsmouth, England.
Having previously been a Scriptwriter he made the move to books in 2022; and has no intention of looking back. https://bio.site/Splatploitation

Printed in Great Britain
by Amazon